Riot Girl

Laura J Whiskens

Also by Laura J Whiskens

Danny Boy

The Entity

Hunter (The Hunter Series)

The Boy (The Hunter Series)

Becoming (The Hunter Series)

Pieces of Me

Telling Tales (Collection of Short Stories)

Coming Soon

C is for Cancer

The Memory Box

My Immortal

Riot Girl

Laura J Whiskens

For the first loves that become the last loves, this is for you.

It's real, I've seen it.

Sally & Richard

Kate & Rich

Hev & Dan

Kelly & Lee

"He smiles at me, and I am suddenly seventeen again - the year I realize that love doesn't follow the rules, the year I understood that nothing is worth having so much as something unattainable."

— *Jodi Picoult, My Sister's Keeper*

Contents

About the Author

Laura J Whiskens was born in 1980's Britain in a council estate full of colourful characters. The youngest of three girls, life was far from dull. She discovered her love of books and writing from a young age and her earliest memories include the wonder of her local library as a Sunday afternoon treat with her stepfather These early days are responsible for her love of all things book-related, including the smell of old book shops and libraries.

In the early days, Laura was horrified at the thought of new-fangled e-readers… until she realised just how many books she could take on holiday with her without exceeding her baggage allowance!

Laura's writing career truly began with a little girl called Cathy and her bestfriend, Danny. In the summer of 2013 Danny Boy was published on Amazon's Kindle store and the short story still receives rave reviews some two years later.

After years of actively trying *not* to write (because writing was an 'impossible' dream, or so she thought), Laura cannot now go a day without a new character popping into her head for a chat (she's not crazy, honest).

Laura now lives in a picturesque country town in Warwickshire with her boyfriend and the cats… because every write has to have a cat–it's in the job description.

www.laurawhiskenswriter.com

Acknowledgements

First and foremost, thank you to my partner Ash for listening to me say "I need to work on my book" a million times a week for almost a year. For supporting me and believing me, and for dragging me along to countless gigs with your old band–thank you.

To my family and friends, who inspire me every day and give me the strength to believe in myself. You mean more to me than I can say.

A huge thank you to all at the Robot Review Club–you have taught me so much and have been such a wonderful support for me. Without you I'd be completely lost in this world we call "indie".

From the same group, a special 'thank you' to Natasha, Shannon and Kyleigh–you spurred me on when I was convinced I wasn't good enough. For your reviews, suggestions and 'you can do its' I will be eternally grateful.

Thank you to the 120 Club for pushing me to write every day, even if it's just a 'to do' list; writing really is an exercise which should be practiced every day otherwise it's hard to get back in the frame of mind to get anything done.

To my late and dear Mum, who's voice is always in the back of my mind urging me on–"Where's the rest of my book?" echoes in my head throughout each new project. I love and miss you every day.

Finally, a thank you to *you*–the reader of my book! Without you I wouldn't still be here, tapping away on this keyboard and publishing this book. Keep reading and reviewing, you make it all worthwhile.

Part One

Indi, Aged Seventeen

CHAPTER ONE

It was not long after my seventeenth birthday that Joel Travis climbed through the window of my bedroom. He entered the trailer that I called home, as he always had, but this time I could sense that it was different. There was a hunger in his deep blue eyes that I had never seen before. The sight made my heart race and my cheeks flush.

The atmosphere was so intense that I didn't dare utter a word in case I broke the spell he was apparently under. My heart was thumping so hard I was sure he'd be able to hear it. We'd been best friends since we were four and I had been in love with him since we were thirteen–almost four whole years of waiting and hoping that he'd open his eyes and realise he loved me too.

"Indi," he said breathily, causing my heart to stop dead.

For a moment I forgot how to breathe. Joel paused for a second as his feet found the bedroom floor and I worried for a moment that he had changed his mind. I needn't have been concerned.

He rushed at me, pulling my body close, kissing me harshly and running his fingers through my long black hair as he pulled my face closer to his own. It was a good thing he was holding me because I didn't trust my legs not to buckle beneath me.

I could have cried with joy and excitement in that moment—which would have been a bad move since my eyes were thick with black eyeliner and my heavily mascara-ed eyelashes would definitely have run.

Crying would not be cool right now and Joel would certainly poke fun at me forever for being such a girl over a kiss. I'd have to keep my rock chick persona in check; I couldn't have her running for cover while the fluffy pink girly girl took over.

Joel backed me over towards my unmade bed; I hoped to God that there were no underwear or teddy bears on there that could ruin the moment. If this was going to be 'it', then I was ready. I loved him, and not in a stupid schoolgirl way. I truly loved him in a real and forever kind of way. I knew everything about him and even the bad stuff only made my feelings for him stronger.

"Is this okay?" he whispered, pulling back to look deep into my eyes as he lay on top of me on the bed, the weight of his body pressing down on me.

I nodded yes, and pulled his t-shirt up over his head with hands shaking in anticipation. This would be my first time, but I wasn't nervous in the way I thought I would be. I ran my hands through his dark, spiked hair and returned his kisses as he slowly undressed me.

I knew Joel well enough to know he'd take care of me. I was pretty sure that this wasn't his first time but it didn't bother me. We were in a band together with two of our close friends–I sang while he played bass guitar and growled obscenities–and after gigs there were usually groupies around, waiting to throw themselves at the guys.

I didn't know what had brought Joel to the trailer that night, and at this point I didn't care much either. All that mattered was that he was here; undressing me and kissing me with a passion I'd dreamt about for the last few years. Adrenalin rushed through my body and I ached for him, pulling him as close as I could.

My dad was out drinking as per usual and my mom had gone AWOL years earlier so we were completely alone in the place I loosely called home.

I lay naked on the bed and Joel drank me in, looking at me in a way he never had before. I felt exposed and suddenly scared; in this moment everything was about to change. Even if I tried, I couldn't go back to pretending he was just my friend.

Joel brought his head level with my own and kissed me softly so that I got goose bumps. My body reacted to him without having to think about it.

"You're beautiful," he touched my pale face softly while his other hand ran down my side and he gently kissed my collarbone.

I didn't know how to respond to that–no one had ever called me beautiful before–so I just kissed him back and allowed my hands to wander down his chest. I'd wondered for a long time how his bare flesh would feel against my own skin. So I allowed my hands to touch all of the places I wouldn't normally be allowed while in the 'friend zone'.

I sat up slowly, feeling braver now, and removed his jeans and boxers. I let out a little gasp as I released him. Joel smiled, a little embarrassed. Even if it wasn't his first time, I guess he must have felt vulnerable too, baring himself so wholly to me. The thought made me feel bolder somehow and I grasped hold of the length of him as I gazed at him, chewing on my bottom lip. He closed his eyes and pushed me back down on the bed.

As he moved into me I bit on my lower lip to stifle a scream. It hurt and I hadn't been expecting that. I didn't have any close girlfriends and the snippets I'd heard from the girls in high school hadn't prepared me for the burning pain between my legs. I was afraid if he saw the pain in my eyes he might stop so I closed my eyes and tried to keep my expression straight.

After that, I lost all logical thought as I gave into the feeling of him.

Afterwards we lay together for a while and for the first time since I'd known him I didn't know what to say to Joel. He, it seemed, felt the same way. Years of my hopes and dreams had led to this exact moment but I hadn't actually considered what might happen if he had opened his eyes and realised what was standing in front of him. Not half an hour earlier I was full of teenage bravado, and now here I was: feeling incredibly conscious of the fact that my naked body was exposed. I thought of ways to gracefully cover myself, none of them were actually possible.

Shit, I thought to myself as I remembered that my dressing gown was on a chair across the room. I'd have to show my ass to him if I went over to get it, and I didn't trust my legs to carry me anyway. In the end I sat up and put a pillow across me, covering as much as I could as I hugged it close to me. Joel sat up and hunched over but didn't bother to cover himself.

"Are you okay?" he asked, not looking at me.

"Yeah, I'm okay." I replied and fidgeted as I found a t-shirt sticking out from my pillow and pulled it on. "Actually… I'm a little confused."

"I'm sorry Indiana." The two words crushed me. He thought the whole thing was a huge mistake; I felt my stomach do a flip and I fought the urge to cry.

My fury was heightened by him using my full name; my parents, both drunks, thought it would be amusing to call me Indiana when I was born. Yeah, nothing wrong with that name... unless your surname is Jones. Indiana Jones–what a joke; it's not like I didn't like the films, but it took years of bitch-slapping to get people to stop teasing me over it.

"Don't be," I replied coolly and pulled on my pants before standing with my back to him.

I couldn't stand the thought of being weak in front of him. So I shut myself off completely; to hell with him anyway.

I was surprised to feel his arms circle me from behind, hugging me with his head coming to rest on my shoulder. My heart fluttered at him being so close, feeling his breath on my neck.

"I'm sorry if it hurt you I meant, I'm not sorry that it happened." How well he knew me after all. The sick feeling subsided.

"How *did* this happen, Joel? I mean, I thought we were just friends? I had no idea..." I trailed off as I turned to look him in the eye. Awkward as it might be, I couldn't help but speak to him like I always had: frankly and without hiding, like I did with almost everyone else.

"It doesn't matter," he avoided my gaze and I felt angry with him. Now he was hiding from me.

"It does matter! You make me so mad!" Joel looked surprised as I flung myself out of his embrace. "Do you know how long I've waited for you?"

"What?" Now he was genuinely confused.

No going back now though, I thought to myself. It was time to get everything out–everything between us was now changed forever anyway.

"Four years Joel, four years I've waited for you to look at me like you did tonight. You're my best friend; you have *no* idea how hard it's been for me to hide my feelings from you. Billy and Waz knew about it a long time ago." Billy and Waz, our best friends, always could see right through me. They'd teased me about my 'crush' a couple of times in the beginning but were more sympathetic as we'd gotten older.

Joel sat back down on the bed, grabbing my hand and practically dragging me down next to him.

"Don't be such a pain. Sit!" Joel laughed and I huffed as I sat down next to him, trying to keep my legs from touching his. "I didn't know, okay? I actually had no idea. We're friends, you're my best friend. I didn't know you felt that way. If I had..."

"Then what? You wouldn't have come here tonight?" My inner riot girl had her spikes out now. I could be such a bitch sometimes.

"Then maybe I would have come here a long time ago, actually," he replied, stroking the side of my face gently with his hand.

My heart skipped and my cheeks flushed. Now I was mad at myself. For years I'd tortured myself for nothing?

"Someone was being a douche, talking about you tonight and I was furious. I punched him in the face and the next thing I know, I'm outside your window." He put his head in his hands and I was about to ask who the hell was talking about me when he grabbed my hand. "I thought about leaving, I really did. I caught sight of you through the curtain and I couldn't stop myself."

"Oh." I didn't know what to say to him, I didn't know how I felt about any of it.

"Honestly, I didn't think I felt anything more for you than friendship. A couple of times when I've seen you speaking to other guys it's pissed me off but I shrugged it off I guess," he carried on. "Like you said, I guess Billy and Waz knew better than I did."

Billy was his brother and Waz our wayward fourth. The two of them would gladly tease us about anything, except for this it would seem. They would often look knowingly at me after gigs when gaggles of pink fluffy girls would gather around Joel, laughing like hyenas even though he hadn't said anything *that* funny.

"I hated girls even looking at you, that's when I started to realise," I revealed. "Then when your dad left and you came over here and fell asleep as I held you, I couldn't stop myself."

The year we turned thirteen Joel and Billy's dad went out to get milk. Their younger sister opened the refrigerator to find a full, unopened bottle sat on the shelf. He didn't come back that night, or any since. When their mom came home she flipped out and got drunk, shouting abuse at her three children. Billy was fourteen but Casey was only seven and seeing her mother that way really hurt her. Joel came over to my trailer once they'd managed to get her to sleep.

He'd climbed through my window and burst into tears; the first time I'd seen him cry since he broke his ankle climbing trees when we were eight. We lay down on my bed and he'd cried himself to sleep in my arms. I'd never loved him more that right there in that moment.

"I always find myself here; whatever goes on, this is where I want to be." He was playing with a strand of my hair.

This week it was jet black all the way through, the week before I had purple streaks through it. I dyed my hair on a whim, most of the time just to see if anyone noticed. Without a mother to tell me off I felt the need to draw attention to myself. Dad never noticed, of course.

"It's a happening place," I joked and bumped my shoulder against his. We were sat there in just t-shirts and our underwear and I was starting to get cold.

"It's you, it's always you," he replied and looked into my eyes again. The passionate look was starting to smoulder in them again.

The spot between my legs was still sore but I was excited in spite of myself. No one had ever looked at me in this way before, and the fact that it was Joel was perfect to me. I smiled as he moved in to kiss me again and before long we were naked once more.

"You guys finally got your acts together then?" Billy said to me as we sat on the field waiting for the others to join us. The sun felt warm on my body but I felt goose bumps as Billy spoke.

I blushed involuntarily, clearly Joel had told him about the night before. He put his arm around my shoulders loosely and we lay back on the grass. I let my head rest on his shoulder as I absentmindedly pulled at the buttercups next to me.

"What did he tell you?" I asked, not entirely comfortable about having this kind of conversation with Billy but too curious not to.

"That you got your freak on." He laughed as I punched him in the arm hard. "Hey! Okay he didn't say it quite like that. He said he finally realised why he got so pissed when he saw other guys look at you and he went over to see you and, you know, stuff happened."

"Was... Was the 'stuff', you know... Okay?" I wished for the ground to swallow me whole, my cheeks burned with embarrassment.

"I don't even wanna know that much detail! You're like my sister for Christ's sake," he grimaced at me and rolled onto his side to look at me as I shifted my head onto the ground. "He had the biggest smile on his face today. He's happy and that's good."

I grinned at him and pushed him back to the ground playfully. I didn't want to have to look him in the eye right now.

"Do you mind?" I asked hesitantly.

Billy and I had never really been a thing but a couple of years ago we got close to it. He said he liked me but I was still holding out for Joel. We'd kissed and I freaked out and we never spoke about it again.

"Nah, of course not. I always kinda knew it was him you liked and I love both of you so if you want to get together then that's okay with me. That whole thing... Well, it's water under the bridge." He looked down at the ground and pulled at the grass, not quite looking me in the eye.

I reached over and squeezed his hand as a thank you. The four of us were so close, if Joel and I being a 'thing' was going to mess with that then I didn't think I could go through with it. Billy was a player, he never admitted to liking girls and I hoped that I hadn't hurt him by only having eyes for Joel, especially since they were brothers.

"Hitting on my girlfriend already bro?" The sound of Joel calling me his girlfriend had my inner cheerleader screaming her head off, pom-poms and all. I inwardly cringed at myself but felt my face light up at the sight of him nonetheless.

He and Waz dropped down on the grass next to us, Joel pulled me to him so my head was resting on his knee. I was way too uncomfortable in front of the other two, who were making kissy faces and crossing their eyes at us.

"Oh my God," I cringed and hid my face. "I hate you both so much right now."

"Get used to it kiddo," Waz smirked at me with a wink. "How do you think we feel watching you guys smooch? Totally, totally wrong."

"They're just jealous," Joel leaned down to kiss me full on the lips. I ducked out of the way. "Playing hard to get?"

"Playing 'oh my God this is too weird in front of dumb and dumber' actually," I replied.

I sat up now and scooted a little way away from Joel. As much as I'd waited for this, I was completely unprepared for how weird it would feel to smooch in front of our little group.

"Nah, she's just come to her senses already bro," Billy laughed and ducked as Joel threw a handful of grass at him. "Come on Waz, let's leave them to it – we can go mess with the Barbie Brigade." Billy was referring to the school cheerleaders who we knew were practising in the school gym.

"Catch you guys later," Waz and Joel fist bumped and he leaned down to ruffle my hair before he and Billy made their way across the field.

"Alone at last," Joel smiled at me and pulled me into a kiss.

This, right here, was me in heaven.

CHAPTER TWO

I stamped the snow off my red biker boots before heading into the lock up. In the months since Joel and I had gotten together winter had edged its way into our lives and now it was freezing cold, so much so that I could now see little clouds of my own breath coming from my mouth. Joel greeted me with a kiss and a big smile, warming me instantly.

I'd thought my dream relationship would have shattered as soon as it became a reality but we were still going strong and I couldn't have been happier. I'd had a bad throat thanks to the turn in the weather and was having to pick up extra shifts at the diner because my dad had had his shifts cut at work so I hadn't made it to many practices lately.

"Ah, she lives! I thought she was just a ghost of the girl we knew," Waz teased as I settled down on the third-hand sofa in front of the kit.

"Ha-ha," I squeaked and coughed.

"Throat's no better?" Billy asked, looking at Joel in concern. We had a gig in just under a week and my voice had no sign of improving. I hadn't managed to sing at all for a few weeks by this point.

"You need to audition someone else guys," I told them. I cut them off as they started to protest. "It's fine – really. I only sang in the first place 'cause you wanted a female lead. The band was always your thing anyway. I've enjoyed it but it's your dream, not mine. Audition, okay?"

They knew it was true. I could carry a tune and they'd wanted a female vocalist to clash with their heavy sound and I was the logical choice since they hated almost every other teenage girl in town at the time. My dream was to be an artist and I'd spent a lot of time designing posters and CD covers for them over the two years the band had been going.

"I don't like it," Joel protested and came to sit on the sofa with me.

"This gig is important man," Billy reasoned with him.

It was true; this was a huge event. Around a dozen bands from the surrounding areas were coming to play which had apparently peaked the interested of a label scout from LA. If all went well on the night one or more of the bands could be invited to audition for the label by the end of the year. It had caused a real buzz around school and suddenly the popular girls found Billy, Waz *and* Joel 'like so awesome', which was both funny (for them) and worrying (for me) at the same time.

"It really is," I agreed. "If you guys got asked to audition it would be incredible. Goodbye Shitsville, hello sunshine!" I hugged myself into Joel and smiled up at him.

This could be our ticket out of here.

"You really think it was okay?" Joel paced back and forth behind the make shift stage, unable to keep still.

"You guys were fricking awesome, truly!" I reassured him for the hundredth time since they'd finished their set. "I'd definitely tell you if it sucked!"

My voice hadn't improved enough to perform and in the end they'd decided against auditioning to replace me. They had instead gone on as a three piece and Billy had sung the vocals I usually did. He'd been incredibly good at it too, despite always insisting that he couldn't sing. I'd never been a spectator of the band before and it was a strange experience not to be up on stage with them. Tonight I was just a groupie like every other girl there; that part I wasn't overly keen on.

"Dude, I think I blew that solo part royally. What was I thinking? We shoulda auditioned," Billy was pacing in opposite directions to his brother and the sight made me smile.

Waz sat on the floor with his back to the wall, roll up in one hand, his head in another not saying a word. I sat down next to him with my legs stretched out in front of him. He rested his head on my shoulder and we watched the brothers pacing together.

"Of course you were no match for me but I think you sang my parts just fine Bill," I smiled at him. The two of them were starting to make me dizzy. "It was weird to just watch, fun though. People were going crazy, I thought I might get squashed when they started moshing!"

Joel came to a standstill beside me and pulled me to my feet, Waz's head was yanked away as I rose. Joel was sweaty from performing and his black t-shirt clung to his muscly arms and chest, his spiked hair was starting to wilt and he looked exhausted but gorgeous. Every inch the rock star, my heart fluttered and I felt my inner cheerleader swoon at him.

"I didn't like you not being up there with us," he kissed me, his hands wondering down to my backside. Performing had an arousing effect on him I'd come to discover over the months we'd been a couple. "I hope your voice is better soon."

"I think my days as a vocalist after over J," I replied in between kisses. Oh God I loved the kissing. "Billy is just too good."

"So you wanna be my groupie instead baby?" He whispered teasingly into my ear. Though being a groupie outraged me, the feeling of his body pressed to mine and his breath on my neck made me desperately wish we were alone.

"Oh geez guys, get a room already!" Billy threw an empty Coke bottle at his brother and I felt my cheeks flush, suddenly mortified.

"Green's not a good look for you bro," Joel winked at me as I moved away from him. He grabbed hold of my hand and pulled me back towards him.

"I can't wait to get you alone," he whispered to me.

Billy shot us both an exasperated look and went back to pacing around the concrete floor. We were silent, the sound of another band finishing their set drifted in.

"You think the scout guy is going to be interested in us auditioning?" Waz finally spoke up.

"Yeah, I'd say he'd be very interested in you auditioning," came a strange voice from the shadow of the stage curtains.

It was the label scout.

"Man I can't believe this!" Billy was practically bouncing off the walls. "Pinch me, I'm dreaming."

Waz obliged and got punched on the arm for it.

"Ow, dude you said to do it!" Waz laughed as he held his injured arm.

The two of them started rolling around the floor play fighting and fooling around. They were beyond excited after talking to the scout.

The scout, Ray, had said he loved their set and the crowd had gone crazy for them, so that basically told him all he needed to know. There were around five hundred people in the audience during the concert that night and that was a good enough number for the scout to decide that this band had what he was looking for.

Ray had left his card with them, taken their details and said he'd be in touch to sort out their flights to California for the record label auditions. They were told to get ready to leave in the next couple of weeks, if all went well they'd be asked to stay to record some demos.

I was feeling apprehensive. I didn't regret my decision to call it a day as the singer but I was now left wondering what exactly this meant for me as the fourth in this group of friends. And as Joel's girlfriend.

"You okay?" Joel pulled me in for a kiss. They were so happy, I wished I could share their joy.

"Yeah, just a little overwhelmed I guess," I replied. "I can't believe this is happening."

"Me either, it's unreal." We watched the others roll around the floor and laughed. "When that guy told us he liked our shit I thought I was dreaming. I mean, California!"

He started kissing my neck but I was too restless to enjoy his attention. I was grateful for the distraction of the others. Teenage hormones threatened to make me cry; what would I do in this dumb ass town without these clowns to keep me sane?

"It'll be cool, like our first holiday together," Joel was nibbling my ear now. His hormones made him permanently horny.

"How so?" I replied and pulled back to look him in the eyes, surprised at his comment.

"I know these guys will be there too and we'll have to be in the studio," he said. "But you and me, we can still have some time to look around, right?"

"Really? You want me to come?"

"I'll be damned if we're going without you!" he looked outraged at the thought. "Until a couple of days ago you were part of the band, just 'cause you're not singing with us anymore doesn't make you any less a part of it."

I was taken aback. I had presumed that they were going to California for the audition without me while he had presumed that I'd be joining them.

I was suddenly sharing their excitement. I wouldn't be left behind after all.

"I'm sorry guys, I can only get the three of you in – we weren't expecting any... *groupies*," Ray told us as we sat on speakerphone with him.

Beside me Joel clenched his fists. It had been a week since the gig and as promised Ray had called so we could iron out the details of the band's audition for the record label.

"Indi isn't a groupie, she's part of the band dude," Joel tried to explain. It was so embarrassing to be sat there listening to them talk about me.

"In what capacity? When I came to see you there were just the three of you on stage?" Ray asked, his patience starting to waver.

"Well – she was, you see..." Billy realised that I wasn't an official part of the band any more. "She was our vocalist, but she had this throat infection so she had to step down because she couldn't hit the notes. I was standing in that night..."

"So is she a part of the band now? Because I gotta tell you boys, I sold you as an all-male three piece. Nothing was mentioned about there being a fourth member, let alone a girl. We can see you in the market as I saw you, I'm not too sure about the set up you're telling me now..."

"No, I'm not in the band anymore," I jumped in. It was no use, and if they tried to argue it they could lose the chance to audition. "If you're sure there's no way I can join the guys then that's how it has to be."

I kissed Joel's hand and smiled at the other two. *It's okay,* I mouthed to them all.

"Sorry honey, no room for passengers in this business I'm afraid. If there was anything I could do, I would," Ray said through the speakerphone. "Maybe if they pass the record's audition we could get you on a bus over to stay while they record the demos."

"Yeah, okay," we said as one in chorus.

"Cool, so I'll courier over your tickets and then meet you at the airport this end with a car," Ray sounded pleased to have settled the argument. "We've gotten you into a hotel right down the street from the studios and there's plenty for you to do while you're here!"

"Thanks dude," Billy spoke into the speaker. "We'll see you then."

Waz clicked the button to end the call and looked at me. "Sorry Ind, that sucks for you."

"It's cool, really." I didn't trust myself not to cry like a child. "I gotta get to my shift; if I'm late again my boss will fire my ass. I'll catch you later."

"I'll walk you," Joel jumped up and fist bumped the other two to say goodbye. "I'll come over to the lockup after to catch up on everything."

"Later guys," Billy replied and jumped up to kiss me on the head. "It sucks you can't come with us."

Joel and I left hand in hand and walked the back street to the diner I waitressed in. We were both quiet for a while.

"I feel really bad; I want you to come so much. I didn't think there would be any problem with it," he pulled me close and put his arm around me as we walked.

I couldn't help myself, tears welled up and I felt really guilty for being so selfish.

"I'm really happy for you, honestly, I'm just feeling sorry for myself," I told him. "What will I do without you guys here? What will I do without *you* here?"

"I'm gonna miss you so bad," he kissed my head. "You know, we could just be there for the two days and they hate us and send us home with a 'thanks but no thanks.'"

"I don't want that – I want them to love you, I *know* they'll love you. If they ask you to stay and record some demos then we'll deal with it when the time comes."

We were almost outside the diner now.

"You guys going to come over when I'm on my break?" I asked as he pulled me in for a hug.

"Yeah, we'll be over for sure. Have a good shift okay," he kissed me and I headed into the diner.

As I walked through to the staff area I took deep breaths to try and stop the tears from falling. My heart hurt and I was terrified of being left behind to rot in this hellhole of a town without the only people I ever cared about.

I met the guys at the lockup after my shift; they were packing up their things ready for the audition. By the time I arrived they'd pretty much packed up every piece of kit they owned. "Just in case," Joel had said.

My stomach flipped as I finished his sentence: *Just in case we don't come back.* I made my way to the far side of the concrete-blocked room towards the sofa Joel was currently occupying.

"You shouldn't mess with that stuff dude," I said, barely managing to hide my disgust as I moved Waz's paraphernalia out of the way with the tip of my biker boots.

"It's cool, I know my limits Ind." Waz smiled up at me as I passed him in a drug-induced stupor.

"There's no talking to him," Joel pulled me down onto his lap and kissed my neck softly.

I watched as Waz lay back on the worn sofa with a faraway look on his face as the drugs pulled him into their grasp.

"He's going to kill himself, I swear to God," Billy's face mirrored my own as he shook his head at our friend.

"I worry about him, you know?" I shrugged at Billy and chewed my bottom lip.

"We'll watch out for him, he'll be okay with us baby," Joel tried to reassure me as he nuzzled my neck.

Billy rolled his eyes at us and carried on watching the music video playing on our old TV set in the lockup.

Joel's words didn't stop the uneasy feeling in the pit of my stomach. We'd pretty much dragged each other up in life with the absence of decent parents. Soon enough they were going to be far away where I couldn't be there to try and talk sense in Waz.

I looked at Billy, then turned to face Joel and tried to remind myself that they could be sensible and that they could never be dumb enough to fall in to the trap of heavy drugs. They'd look out for Waz. I knew they would.

CHAPTER THREE

I lay with my head against the cool linoleum floor, the toilet just in front of me. My long dark hair sprayed around my on the floor, my natural roots were showing but I didn't have the energy to care. It had been almost four weeks since the guys had left for their audition and Joel had called me two days later, his voice full of excitement and hope for the future.

"They really liked us Indi," he'd told me. "They asked us to stay and record a demo and we said yes! It's unbelievable here; I can't wait for you to see it. Look, I can't stay on for long because they're taking us out but I'll call soon to let you know when you can come."

He'd hung up full of joy and I'd promptly burst into tears. About a week after that I'd started throwing up – morning, noon and night. I'd lost so much weight that I could see my ribs poking through, my skin barely hiding the skeleton of my body.

This morning I'd already spent several hours puking my guts up and the cold floor felt so good against my hot forehead. I couldn't understand what was making me so sick. I'd hardly eaten in days and the smell of the food at work had been unbearable. Thanks to an alcoholic father I hardly ever drank so that wasn't causing my illness either.

My stomach lurched once more and I jumped up to position myself over the toilet bowl for the hundredth time that morning. It was so gross.

"Indiana!" my father yelled through the bathroom door. "You better clean up after yourself!"

"Sure Dad," I yelled back between wretches. "I have enough practice cleaning up after your mess!" I didn't listen to his response; I was too busy with my head in the toilet.

I glared at the cashier as I pushed the flat, white box across the counter towards her, daring her to say a single word to me about what was inside it. For the briefest moment she had a surprised look on her face but it was gone in an instant, replaced with a false smile across her red lipsticked mouth.

Her name badge read 'Heather'; she lived one block away from the trailer park and I knew her face but I never knew her name until now. Heather was now the first person who knew I could be pregnant – in my mind I was wondering if she'd tell anyone; did she even know my name? This time tomorrow would half the school know Indiana (inside I rolled my eyes at the name) Jones, Trailer Trash, was pregnant?

I handed over my money and took the paper bag, shoving it into my coat pocket to conceal my secret a little while longer. Embarrassingly, at the age of seventeen, it had taken weeks of puking before it finally clicked that I could be pregnant. Joel and I hadn't always been careful; we'd actually been cocky enough to think we were invincible against such things as pregnancy.

As I walked back to the trailer my body felt heavy; it felt as if I were walking to my doom. I'd feel a lot better if Joel were here but it had been ten days now since he'd last called and I felt so alone that there was a constant dull ache in my chest where my heart should be.

Back home in the bathroom I tore the box open and devoured the instructions inside. Gross, I had to pee on the stick and that could not be hygienic, surely? As I jiggled about trying to get the right angle for the stick a wave of fury swept over me.

As much as I missed Joel and the others I was also angry with them. How could they just ditch me here without a word? I never thought they'd just forget me. I'd been optimistic to begin with – I thought that they'd send bus tickets for me to join them as soon as they knew they'd be staying away from this hellhole.

Once I'd counted the seconds I pulled out the stick and set it down on some tissue paper while I waited for the results. I paced the bathroom floor then started organising the bottles of shampoo and body wash as I counted the two minutes away. Taking a deep breath I sat on the closed toilet lid and turned the test over in my hands.

Positive.

"What's gotten into you, Indiana?" Beth, the head waitress, shook her head at me as I swept up the remains of a third glass that afternoon. "You're never usually this clumsy!"

Luckily for me a customer caught her attention and she left me knelt down on the floor with the dustpan and brush. My slim frame was struggling to hide the small swelling on my stomach now and I was grateful that no one ever really paid me any attention or people would have started wondering why I was wearing such oversized clothes lately.

"That's coming out of your pay check Indi!" Hank called over to me and I rolled my eyes at him. "That girl has messed up more in one shift than she has in two years of working here."

"Give the kid a break, Hank, she looks exhausted." Hank's pal Jim had a point. I *was* exhausted.

"I'm okay thanks Jim-and I'll pay for the glass Hank," I replied. "I'm just a little distracted with school work today, that's all."

That was only a half lie; I couldn't remember the last time I'd handed in an assignment. If I wasn't careful the school would start sending letters home to my dad about it. That would set alarm bells ringing. I'd always been a high achiever at school. It's easy to get good grades when no one expects anything of you.

Hank looked over at the chrome clock above the counter. "Go on home kiddo, it's almost the end of your shift anyway. Indiana Jones here is gonna be famous one day, she's smart you know."

I rolled my eyes at him again but with a playful smile. "Thanks boss. There's more to life than fame though-just getting out of this town will do me fine."

I went out back to the staff changing room and slipped out of my turquoise blue waitressing dress and into black jeans and an over-sized shirt over my black vest top. The jeans were starting to cut into my stomach now so I sucked my gut in to do the top button up.

"Getting a little bit of a gut there, 'riot girl'," I flinched at the nickname and the thought of being watched as I changed. I turned to find Hank's nephew, Daniel, standing behind me.

The nickname came from my fiery temper. I had been known to cause chaos when people got on the wrong side of me, which wasn't too often these days. Once word got around that I was small but feisty and had a good right hook, people tended to keep their distance.

"I'm pretty sure lurking in corners watched girls get undressed is an offense, you filthy peeping Tom!" I slung my apron at him in disgust.

"I was sitting here waiting to start my shift, *Indiana*," he smirked. "So what's with the gut?"

"What's with your face? You look like road kill," I spat back venomously before storming out of the room, slamming the door as I went.

Daniel was a jock and a jerk. He'd been vile to me since forever and he hated Joel and the others with a passion. He liked to taunt me now with the nick name 'riot girl' just to remind me that they'd ditched me and then left me behind in this godforsaken town with no one to back me up when there was trouble. Not that I needed any reminding.

I couldn't believe he'd sat there watching me change without making himself known. I shuddered as I thought of his eyes all over my body as I stripped down to my underwear unknowingly. And he'd seen my stomach; he wasn't the kind of guy to keep his mouth shut and let it drop either. He'd taunt me about getting fat just for the fun of it. I just hoped he didn't suddenly grow an IQ and figure out I wasn't fat but pregnancy making my stomach swell.

"Clearly something's wrong with you, riot girl," Daniel had been bugging me all shift and was starting to really test my patience.

I carried on wiping the tables down as he followed me around the diner like a puppy, as had become his habit since his peeping Tom act.

"You are seriously starting to piss me off," I hissed at him, "and quit it with that stupid nickname already."

"You love it," he smiled, mischief twinkling in his green eyes.

If he wasn't such a douche he might be quite nice to look at. I shook the thought from my mind; apart from Joel I'd never been the kind of girl to notice if a guy was attractive or not. The thought was alien to me, especially in people who annoyed me as much as this jerk.

"Shut up," I threw the cloth I'd been using at him and went back behind the counter. It had been a quiet afternoon and there were just the two of us out front. I pulled my textbook and notepad out from behind the cash register to carry on with my homework. Hank was okay with the school staff doing their assignments when it was quiet, as long as the tables were clean and customers tended to.

"That should have been in last week," he leaned over me, his face close to my own so that I could see the splatter of freckles across his nose.

"Jeez, personal space please!" I pushed him away so there was a good foot of space between us. "I wasn't well, Mr Bailey gave me an extension okay?"

"I can help if you want," he shrugged nonchalantly. "I got a B but it's better than a fail."

I looked at him sceptically, but there was no teasing look on his face. He seemed genuine and to be honest I was getting a little desperate now that I was falling so far behind with my work. When I didn't object he pulled my book towards him and leaned against the counter to read what I'd written out so far.

We spent the rest of the shift going through that assignment and revision for a test we had the next day. He even resisted the urge to use my nickname, and as much as he annoyed me, he really did help.

CHAPTER FOUR

On my break I retreated to the staff changing room; no one tended to go in there except for the start and end of each shift so I knew I'd be alone for a while. I needed to get the weight off my feet and sit down for a while; there were some tatty old chairs stored in there which weren't fit for the front of the diner anymore so I settled in one of those.

"So, who's the daddy?" I spun around to find Daniel leaning against the doorframe, his arms crossed with a serious look on his face.

"I don't know what you're talking about," I replied curtly and turned away from him, closing my eyes and praying for him to just go away.

"Don't play dumb with me Indi."

It occurred to me that this was the first time he'd used my name at the beginning of a conversation. He normally started off with 'riot girl' in order to get my back up, something he took real pleasure in doing.

"Please, just leave me alone Daniel," I pleaded, turning back to face him.

He closed the staffroom door and came to sit on a chair beside me; the stuffing was protruding from the blood red faux leather base.

"I don't want to upset you Indi," he said earnestly. "I just want to help you, if I can."

Daniel looked me right in the eye and he seemed so sincere that, in spite of myself, I found myself wanting to confess all. I rested my hands on the swelling of my stomach, visible through my turquoise blue uniform now that I was seated, and gently moved my palms along the curve of the bump.

"Does it... kick?" he asked quietly, eying the bump cautiously.

"Yeah, it moves a lot now," I replied with a small smile playing on my lips. This was the first time I'd spoken out loud about the baby and it felt nice. "At first it just felt like little butterflies fluttering around inside, but now the movements are big."

Daniel lifted his hand tentatively, looking at me with raised eyebrows in a silent request for permission to touch my stomach. I hesitated for a moment before nodding yes.

The baby was wriggling around and so I took Daniel's hand and moved it to a spot just left of my belly button, where the baby was practicing kicking footballs. The moment his hand rested there the baby kicked hard and Daniel shot out of his seat in surprise.

"Are you scared of a little kick?" I couldn't help but laugh at him; I'd never seen Daniel so flustered by something before now.

"Of course not," he tried to regain his composure and sat back down, although with a little more space between the two of us this time around. "So, who is the father?"

I didn't want to answer him; in truth it was because I felt so foolish. How could I admit to him that the father had just upped and left me and hadn't bothered to return my calls in months now?

A heavy silence hung between us; although we'd been spending more time together at work over the last few weeks, we didn't really know each other. We barely acknowledged each other at school; if we passed we would say 'hi' but then we'd lose ourselves in the crowded halls as though the exchange had never happened. Daniel just wasn't someone I'd ordinarily share my secrets with. Just a couple of months earlier I'd have told him to take a long walk off a short cliff if he'd have even breathed in the same room as me.

"What does it matter?" I shrugged.

"It *does* matter Indi- does he even know?" Daniel replied, his face set in a serious expression once more.

His concern made the corners of my mouth turn up a little; it was quite sweet that he was so troubled about the baby and I.

"No, he doesn't know-but it isn't from lack of trying to tell him," I sighed heavily and shrugged my shoulders.

"It's that guy from the band, right? Joel. The guy who got signed? I used to see you guys hanging out together around school," Daniel rested his elbows on his knees and looked up at me from his hunched over position.

It was strange; Joel, Billy and Waz had been my whole life, yet Daniel barely knew their names, let alone their faces. It surprised me that Daniel had noticed us together-he'd always seemed so self-involved.

"I don't want this getting out, do you understand?" I'd dropped my guard for too long, Daniel was getting under my skin and learning my secrets and I didn't like it.

"Hey, I'm not going to say anything, alright?" he replied earnestly. "So, he's not returning your calls?"

"I'm sure he's just really busy out there. Being signed is a huge deal, you know? The label is probably keeping them tied up. He'll call, eventually."

I found myself trying in vain to defend the actions of an eighteen-year old guy who'd been whisked off to play rock-star. Of course he hadn't called, why would he? His silence was unforgiveable, but also understandable.

He was in a whole new world now, why would he want his past dragging him down? He'd probably met some leggy blonde model by now and forgotten all about me; a lump lodged in my throat at the thought of Joel with someone else.

"Why don't you go see him, make him listen?" Daniel said softly, aware of the tears threatening to spill down my cheeks.

The same question had been bugging me since I first took the pregnancy test. I'd desperately wanted to get on the first bus out of town and go find my best friend and tell him about the stupid mess I'd gotten in to. That *we'd* gotten in to.

"I don't have the money to pay for the bus fare," I confessed. "I've been taking extra shifts here to try and pay for it. The guys were supposed to send a ticket for me if they got signed, but I guess they forgot about it."

Daniel looked at me, the pity in his eyes was clear. Ordinarily it would have made my inner riot girl kick off, but I was just too exhausted to care now.

"I don't suppose you'd let me help you out?" he asked.

"And how do you propose to do that?" I replied.

"I could loan you the money for your ticket," he shrugged.

"No way! You and I, we're not even friends, why would you want to loan me money?" I was shocked at the suggestion, my eyes wide as I spoke.

"I kinda thought that we *were* friends, or at least getting there Indi." He actually looked a little hurt, which made me feel bad.

I thought back over the past few weeks and realised he was right. Gone was the sense of irritation and loathing each time he walked into the same room as me. Instead, I found myself glad to have him around. He made our shared shifts go quicker and we'd gotten into the habit of clearing up early so we could get our school assignments done together before closing time at the diner. And, true to his word, he *had* kept my pregnancy secret so far.

"I guess you're right, we sort've have fallen into being friends, haven't we? I hadn't even realised it until now," I replied with a genuine smile.

He returned the smile, but his was teasing. "I knew you couldn't resist my charm forever."

Daniel jumped up quickly, narrowly avoiding the punch I'd thrown at his arm. As he left the room, heading back to work, I heard him call out to me–

"Come on, Riot Girl–break's over, you're late!"

This time I smiled at the nickname. For the first time since The Riots had left, I didn't feel quite so alone.

Several weeks had passed since our conversation in the staffroom and Daniel and I had started to share the occasional lunchtime together at school. Only when his goon friends weren't around, of course. He approached me the first few times, I would never have dreamed of trying to extend our new-found friendship to school. We'd gotten a few strange looks: me in my oversized rock t-shirts, jet black hair and heavily pencilled eyes and Daniel in his chinos and perfectly styled locks. But he hadn't seemed to notice, or if he had, he didn't seem to care.

When I finally found him in the lunch hall he was sitting alone, as I had hoped. It was a relief that his jock buddies and their girlfriends weren't around, I'd been hoping to speak to Daniel and we weren't on shift together that night. I slid into the chair opposite him and pulled out my lunch bag, barely able to contain my smile as I tried to be indifferent to him.

"My God-is that, no. It simply cannot be," Daniel mocked me. "Is Indiana Jones s*miling*?"

I shot him a look and he laughed at me.

"Hey buster, I can fix that face of yours, ya know?" I threatened him playfully.

He knew by now that I hated people using my full name, and so he gleefully alternated between that and 'riot girl'. At first it had really pissed me off, but the more he did it the less I started to mind. I think that bugged him, which was a bonus.

"Yeah, yeah. I'm terrified, can't you tell?" Daniel took a bite of his cheeseburger and looked at me with a knowing smile. "So what's put that smile on your face?"

My stomach grumbled at the sight of his lunch, I ignored it and leaned across the table conspiratorially.

"I have the money," I whispered; Daniel looked confused so I continued. "You know, for the bus ticket to California!"

Daniel's smile faltered slightly for the briefest of moments, so quick that I thought I might have imagined it.

"Oh, so when are you going?" he asked, taking another bite out of his burger.

"Next Friday, after last period," I eyed his burger. It looked a lot tastier than my ham salad on brown. "Dad won't even notice, and I'll pass a note to say I'm sick for the couple of days of school I'll miss."

It was missing school that made me anxious. I didn't want to fall behind after working so hard through all of this to keep up. Daniel pushed his fries over to me and I gratefully accepted. The baby liked greasy food in spite of my best efforts to be healthy during the pregnancy and Daniel knew it.

"You're a real rebel you know, Indi. You're basically running away from home, but you won't cut your last class? And I'll bet you're hating the thought of missing a couple of days school too, aren't you?" Daniel shook his head and laughed gently at me. "You're a real puzzle, you know?"

"Cut class?" I feigned horror. "Never! And actually, yes, I'm not looking forward to missing school, okay? If I could wait until I could pay for a plane ticket, I would but 'it' would be in high school by then."

I pushed my apple across the dining table to him and he picked it up, sinking his teeth into the luscious flesh of it while I pushed a handful of fries into my mouth with a smile.

"Thanks," he said.

"You need to eat more fruit, it's good for you," I said with a mouthful of greasy fries.

"Yes ma'am," he rolled his eyes playfully. "Just make sure you call me when you get there, okay? Call me at the diner so I know you're safe."

"Yes sir," I smiled.

I turned to wave goodbye as I boarded the bus; Daniel had insisted on driving me to the station. He made his hand into a mime-phone, gesturing for me to remember to call him and I nodded in response.

He'd loaned me his Walkman and I'd loaded the front pocket of my backpack with tapes to listen to on the trip. Tucked away in the larger compartment of my bag was a book and assignment from English class. Rebel indeed, I thought to myself. Daniel had even put together some food for me from the diner. He was such a worrier.

Under normal circumstances I might think he was cute; but these were definitely not normal circumstances, the movement in my stomach reminded me.

The bus pulled away and I took one last look back at him. I was a little sad. If things worked out the way I'd hoped, I might not see Daniel again.

I settled back in my seat and felt a light tap on my shoulder.

"When are you due, honey?" a grey-haired lady smiled kindly and nodded to my stomach.

I was a little taken aback; no one at home had noticed-even my own father-but this stranger had taken one look at me and spotted the pregnancy right away.

"I have ten weeks left," I rubbed my belly with a smile before settling in for the long ride ahead.

I arrived at the record label building in the early afternoon. I was tired and my clothes were crumpled but I was relieved to have finally arrived.

My relief was short lived after being taken into a side room by a guy who called himself Paulie. He was apparently The Riots manager now

I'd spent the last ten minutes trying to explain that Roy, the scout, had arranged with Joel and the others to send for me once they'd signed to the label. I'd told him that Joel had promised he would send me a bus ticket so I could join them out here.

"Listen honey, I'm sure that he made all kinds of promises to you, but that was before he came to LA! This is no place for a nice girl like you, and at this point in his career it's no place for a girlfriend."

"But please, it's important," I pleaded with him. "I can't get through on the number Ray gave me and I *have* to speak to Joel."

He looked me up and down and sighed.

"Sweetheart, this is California. They've got no time for girlfriends, or babies." He put his hand into his inner jacket pocket and pulled out a roll of notes. "Take this, and take care of *it* – for everyone's sake."

Paulie pushed a wad of crisp notes in my hand and walked away down the corridor. I placed a hand on my swollen belly. I was eighteen, thirteen weeks pregnant and I had just risked life and limb to hitchhike half way across the country to come here, to the label offices, after failing to get hold of any of the boys.

The guys had left twelve weeks earlier and had been signed immediately after they'd auditioned. In the first couple of weeks I'd gotten three or four calls a week; sometimes from Joel on his own, sometimes from the three of them from their hotel room.

After I'd started throwing up into the third week and feeling dizzy, I tried to call the hotel they'd been staying at and was told that they'd moved on. Thanks to a helpful receptionist I knew that the studio had set them up with a small apartment because they'd agreed to stay on in California to work with the label's management team, but Paulie had refused to tell me where the apartment was.

I was positively furious with Joel. How could he just leave me? How could they all have just forgotten me like this?

I felt light-headed. It had taken just over two days to get here, jumping from bus to bus on my travels. It had been almost a day since I'd last had anything to eat or drink. I looked down at the money in my hand; there must have been a few hundred bucks there. I balled my hand into a fist and cried tears of anger and frustration.

I knew that there was no way I was going to get past this wall of people to get to the guys; not in this 'condition', they probably had pregnant teens traipsing in and out of the place all the time in their line of work. Drug fuelled parties and drunken orgies–pregnant girls were a dime a dozen in rock star land.

I thought over what Paulie had said to me–*'Take care of it.'* I knew exactly what he meant, but I didn't know if I had the courage to go through with that, not by myself. It was way too late for an abortion anyway, and I had wanted to talk it over with Joel before I decided whether or not to go through with adoption.

I'd come here to speak to Joel, my best friend and father of this child growing inside me, and ask him what to do. I couldn't make the decision about its life without talking to him first. I wiped my eyes on my shirtsleeve and resigned myself to the knowledge that I'd be leaving here without doing that.

After an exhausting, frightening journey over here, I would be leaving just a couple of hours after arriving. I'd get some food, for the baby's sake–though I felt too sick to eat in all honesty–and then I'd get a bus home. Paulie was paying, after all.

CHAPTER FIVE

I sat on the bus on the way home in a numbed state. I was afraid that if I allowed myself to feel anything that I'd break down in tears and I wouldn't be able to stop myself from falling apart.

Paulie's words kept playing on my mind. I didn't know if I could just give my baby away. He or she was all that I had now. The thought of abandoning it like my mother had done to me made me sick to my stomach.

Joel had left me-Billy and Waz too-and it stung. They'd been my best friends, my family, and we had gone through thick and thin together, until now. They had simply forgotten me.

It had been more than six months since I'd had so much as a phone call from Joel. I had genuinely believed that he loved me, or at the very least that our friendship had meant something, even if our relationship had been a complete lie.

Now I had to go back home with my tail between my legs. Thank God that only Daniel knew where I had been; that in itself was humiliating enough, without anyone else knowing.

I would have to tell my dad about the pregnancy now, and the school guidance counsellor, Miss Smith. There was no avoiding it any longer, it was time to confess to my stupidity and deal with the fall out of it all.

My stomach did a flip, which had nothing at all to do with the baby.

We met at the park and sat on the grass in the late evening sun. Daniel listened to my tale with disgust and surprise, just as a good friend should.

"They wouldn't even let you speak to him?" he was outraged for me. "What assholes!"

"Nope; so the whole thing was a complete waste of time and money," I replied, wiping a tear from my face. "And I'm still no wiser about what to do. I did come to the conclusion that it's time to tell people though, my Dad included."

"I can't believe no one's noticed already," he admitted, putting a protective arm around my shoulder. "Those shirts shouldn't be fooling anyone, least of all your own dad."

I looked down at my faded black Aerosmith t-shirt and shrugged. "No one ever noticed me before, why would they start now?"

"I noticed you," he said quietly, retracting his arm and looking at his hands self-consciously.

There was an uncomfortable silence and I noticed that Daniel's cheeks had the faintest pink blush across them.

"So. Who are we going to tell first?" he asked, to break the silence.

"We?" I replied, eyebrows raised questioningly.

"Yes, we. You don't think I'm going to let you go through this part on your own do you?" he took my hand in his own and squeezed it gently. "You're my friend and you need me, whether you'll admit it or not Indi."

"You don't need to do this Daniel, you don't owe me anything," I argued. "No one has to know you were even aware of the pregnancy."

"I want to. I hate the idea of you having to face these judgemental assholes on your own; it's just not right," he replied stubbornly.

I was conscious that he was still holding onto my hand; I was even more conscious of the fact that I didn't actually mind. It felt surprisingly comforting that Daniel, of all people, had my back. I just wondered when and how our unlikely friendship had blossomed from mild irritation to this.

I squeezed his hand back. "Thank you. You really don't have to do this, you know."

"I know. But I want to; as long as that's okay with you." He smiled and bumped my shoulder with his own.

We stood in Miss Smith's office. She was the school guidance counsellor. She had hardly spoken as I had confessed my pregnancy secret.

She finally broke her silence.

"How irresponsible of you Indiana; you're not planning to keep it, surely?" the disapproval dripped from her words.

Miss Smith was a round, middle-aged woman who had never married or had children of her own. With her life experience, or lack of, I wondered how she was qualified to give guidance. Her greying hair was pulled back into a low, tight bun and her pale blue eyes were watching me with a look of disdain.

"It's my baby," Daniel spoke up, causing my jaw to fall open in shock. "Indi and I plan to keep it, giving it away isn't an option."

I was vaguely aware of being swept up into Daniel's lie, although I wasn't quite sure where it had come from or where it was heading.

Daniel took hold of my hand, gripping it tightly as a show of unity-or, possibly to stop me from falling down in shock.

"Daniel, bringing up a baby is a life changing decision," the guidance counsellor replied. "There are other options for people in your position."

"We made this baby, we'll be the ones to bring it up," he insisted while I stood there like a human goldfish, my jaw bobbing open and shut in an attempt to find my voice. "That's all there is to it."

"Right, well we need to call both of your parents and arrange a meeting," she said. "Arrangements need to be made for Indiana's schooling. Indiana?"

"Uh?" was all I could manage in response.

"Sit down, dear-you look very pale. I'll get you some water and arrange for your parents to be called," she pulled out a chair for me and I fell into it gratefully. "Stay here both of you, I'll be back in a few minutes."

She glided out of the room and the door clicked shut behind her. We waited a few moments before speaking.

"What the hell?" My voice returned at last. "What were you thinking?"

"I'm sorry Indi, I was thinking on my feet," he looked quite pale himself. "If they knew you were on your own, that the father is gone, then they'd push you into giving it up. If it's both of us together they'll back off."

"But your parents!" I felt sick to my stomach, all of the ways this could go horribly wrong were rushing through my mind.

"I know," he groaned. "But it's done now, we'll have to ride this out. There's no going back, okay?"

I paused to think. What choice did I have? Daniel was right, they'd push and push until I felt I had no choice but to give the baby up. But with a father by my side they'd have to listen to what we wanted. The fact that Daniel wasn't actually the father was just a technicality at this stage; we'd work the details out later.

"Okay, you're crazy but okay," I agreed.

We sat in horrified silence as we waiting for her to return and tell us our parents were on the way. I wondered if my dad would bother to come. He'd never been called to school about me before; I wondered what would be going through his mind on the way here.

The thought of announcing my pregnancy to him made my head spin. He'd be angry, I knew, but I fantasised that for once he'd be the father I wanted and needed instead of telling me I was a disappointment and no better than my mother.

And Daniel's parents! I knew of them, of course. In a town as small as this I'd have been hard pressed not to have seen them around. They were quite well-to-do and lived on the nice side of town in a beautiful big house with preened gardens. I imagined his mother fainting when she was told her precious son had gotten a piece of trailer trash knocked up.

"Your mother..."

"She'll faint, for sure," he finished my sentence with a small smile.

I laughed; I couldn't help it. It must have been hysteria, or hormones. Daniel joined in and before long tears were streaming down my face as I gasped for breath. We must have looked like lunatics when the guidance counsellor finally returned.

CHAPTER SIX

"Oh my, Daniel!" Daniel's mother, Rebecca, cried out, her hands flying to her mouth with dramatic flair. Her perfectly styled blonde hair was cemented with hairspray and her manicured hands screamed: "stay at home wife".

Daniel's father, James, helped her into a seat before she fell down; he was a handsome older clone of his son with grey hair starting to creep across his brown mop of hair. James hadn't had a lot to say so far, he was apparently the strong and silent type, taking it all in stride. But there was a lot going on in his head, I could see it in his eyes.

"I'm sorry, Ma," Daniel looked genuinely upset and I felt a pang of guilt to be the cause of their distress. "Indi and I, we didn't plan this. But it's happened and we would like to keep our baby, it feels like the right thing to do."

Our baby, I thought. The lie rolled so easily off his tongue; I wanted to confess- to tell them all that this was really Joel's baby and that Daniel was just trying to help me. I couldn't understand how this had escalated so quickly.

"Oh my," Rebecca repeated breathily. "What will people say?"

Miss Smith nodded sympathetically, her duty to her two students temporarily forgotten as she revelled in the drama unfolding around her.

"She's not keeping it, not while she lives under my roof," my father growled, speaking for the first time since he'd arrived. He reeked of stale alcohol and cigarettes.

If we hadn't been in a room full of people he might have tried to hit me; as it was, he was barely keeping his anger under wraps. I shifted uncomfortably, suddenly aware of both the physical and emotional differences between my father and Daniel's.

"People will think what they want to think," James finally spoke up, drawing the surprised attention of everyone in the room. He had a quiet, determined tone. "And Indiana and our grandchild will *not* live under your roof, Mr Jones."

Daniel's face transformed, confusion causing his brow to wrinkle. "Dad?"

"The apartment over my office has been gathering dust, we can set the three of you up in there," James continued. "But, there is one condition."

Rebecca and my father looked at James in something like horror-or perhaps utter shock.

"What's that Dad?" Daniel looked paler than his mother by now; clearly he hadn't been expecting this reaction any more than his mother or I were.

"You must *both*," he said pointedly, looking from Daniel to myself, "finish school, and- if God willing you get the grades- you will both go to college. You will need your education if you want to give this child the life it deserves; that you deserve."

I stared at James in disbelief, my mouth hanging open in surprise. I glanced briefly at my own father, who was glaring at me with pure hatred. I knew that James had his own law firm, a small local business with a two-storey building in the middle of town. I presumed that the apartment must be above his offices.

Daniel looked at me and gave a small nod before turning to his parents. He stepped forward tentatively before embracing James; I thought that I heard him give a small sob but he was standing with his back to me so I couldn't be sure.

"I expect you to provide for your family Daniel," his father stepped back and looked Daniel right in the eye. "Your mother and I will help you but you'll need to learn to manage school with your job alongside the baby. It's going to be hard work, son, especially once you're both in college. But if you want this, truly want it, then we will help all that we can."

Rebecca sobbed into a tissue that Miss Smith had passed to her; she was no doubt worried about what her friends from the tennis club would say. My father stormed out of the room, slamming the office door behind him.

I felt overwhelmed and abandoned by the only family I had left, and I burst into tears. I was embarrassed about crying in front of people I barely knew, but I couldn't stop it. Tears streamed down my face as Daniel embraced me; it felt awkward and I found myself hoping that his parents and Miss Smith didn't pick up on it. After all, we were supposedly in a relationship and expecting a baby together, a hug shouldn't be awkward between two people who were meant to know each other intimately.

Mostly I was overcome with emotion at the understanding and incredible generosity of Daniel's father, but I also had an undeniable feeling of drowning in this web of lies. I felt trapped by it all and out of control of, not only my own life, but that of my baby's.

But if I confessed now, what would happen? Where would I go? My dad had made it clear that I couldn't go back to live at the trailer if I wanted to keep my baby.

And, in spite of the overwhelming fear, I *did* want to keep my baby.

Daniel and his father positioned themselves outside my bedroom door at the trailer; they reminded me of the bouncers I'd seen outside bars in town. My father was sat on our tatty, threadbare couch with a can of beer in his hand and a glare in his eyes aimed firmly at the other two men.

I sighed and clicked my bedroom door shut behind me. I looked around, taking it all in: the window through which Joel had climbed countless times since we were little kids; the bed where we had first made love; the cupboard I'd hidden in as a child when my father was in a rage.

I sat at the end of my bed, still unmade from the last time I'd slept in it a few days earlier. I took a long deep breath, running my bed sheet through my hand and thinking of that first time with Joel, the look in his eyes.

This messy little room contained my life. Not just the material possessions, but so many of my memories. I stood up and started to load my things into bags.

From under my bed I pulled out a worn photo album. It contained the only pictures I had of my mother, hidden away from my father in case he threw them out, and photographs of Billy, Joel, Waz and I as we grew up. They were still precious to me, even if it was too painful to look at them now.

When I'd finished packing everything up I took one final look around the room, my eyes lingering on the window- hoping against the odds that he might appear- and I blinked back the tears I refused to shed over him.

"I'm ready," I called out to Daniel and James.

Daniel's father, ever the old-fashioned gentleman, had been insistent that I was not to lift anything because in my 'condition' I needed to be careful. James and Daniel came into the room and took the bags; when the room was clear I motioned for them to wait for me outside so I could speak to my Dad alone.

"It's okay," I nodded to Daniel, who looked less than impressed about leaving me alone with my father.

"Yeah, it's okay-run along you little shit," Dad spat out venomously as I closed my eyes and shook my head. "Leave me alone with my daughter."

"Dad, don't be such an asshole!" I scolded. "Daniel, please go, I'll be out in a minute."

He turned to leave and joined his father right outside the front door, leaving me alone but not *too* alone. I sighed; it was hard to imagine not living here anymore. Yes, it wasn't the perfect home and I didn't have the greatest dad, but these things were mine and they were all I'd known. I was eighteen-years-old now but I had never imagined leaving home in these circumstances. I was afraid of the unknown path waiting for me outside the front porch of this trailer.

"Don't drink yourself to death, okay?" I spoke softly, sad to be leaving even if he was a drunk. "I'm only in town, if you need me."

"I don't need *you* or anyone," he replied, refusing point blank to look at me.

I nodded and turned to leave.

"Indi," Dad called, and I stopped hopefully. "That Warren boy's mother left an envelope for you."

"She did? When?" My heart raced with the possibility waiting inside that envelope. "Where is it?"

He pointed to the kitchen counter; I moved some things and found it, a white beer-stained envelope.

"Left it a day or so ago–she said the other kids' mom left it for you before she moved," he grunted.

"Billy and Joel's mom? Moved where?" I quizzed him urgently as I ran my fingers across the white stained paper. My heart was fluttering, what was inside it?

"How would I know?" he snapped. "Somethin' about those boys of her getting her a house, outta this godforsaken town."

"They moved her away?" I didn't understand, but it seemed that they'd been in contact with everyone back home except for me.

Dad turned his attention back to the horse racing on TV, no longer listening to me and drawing our exchange to a close.

I tucked the envelope carefully into my pocket. I wanted to keep it out of sight until I got some time alone to find out what was inside.

Part Two

Indi, Aged Twenty-Four

CHAPTER SEVEN

Dreaming of coming home to you; talking like we used to do..."

The melody coming from the radio caused me to stop wiping the table, it was an old song and I wasn't expecting to hear it. My breath caught and my heart hammered against my chest. My legs almost buckled beneath me as the voices on the radio penetrated my defences.

I absolutely hated it when they caught me off guard like that. The lyrics opened up a door I had tried hard to keep locked for so many years. I barricaded my heart and head with every emotional block I could muster but it was times like this, when I was least expecting it, that they managed to catch me unaware and I was seventeen years old once more.

Talking like we used to do my ass, I thought angrily and took it out on the table as I continued to wipe away breadcrumbs and ketchup marks. My little boy was such a messy eater, too much like his father sometimes. I stopped myself before the tears started to roll down my cheeks and instead I thumped the radio power button. The room became quiet, which was worse because then I was left to go over the memories once more; I pushed my cherry-red hair out of my eyes.

Sitting down at the table I closed my eyes, took a deep breath and allowed the images to roll freely through my mind for the first time in a long time. I would have time to pull myself together before anyone else came home. At twenty-four years of age, I still fell to pieces at the thought of my teenage years. I'd tried desperately to mend my broken heart, but all I'd managed to do was crazy glue it back together.

If I'd known when I was seventeen-years-old that letting Joel Travis into my room, and my heart, would be the end of me, I would have thought twice. Still, I couldn't help but think back to that first night and recall the look in his eyes as he took me in his arms...

The front door slammed shut and I came out of my daydream instantly. Looking at the clock on the kitchen wall I was surprised to see that I had been sitting there for more than an hour. The hurt and upset I'd felt after hearing the song was gone and I was horrified to find I was aroused instead. I hardly ever thought about my 'first time' and I'd forgotten how painful I had found it in the beginning. It was the thought of running my hands over Joel's young, lean body that had gotten me hot under the collar; damn him for still being able to get under my skin.

"You okay? You look a little flushed." Daniel said as he came over to kiss me on the head by way of hello. It was lunchtime and I hadn't gotten his sandwich ready which seemed to have put him off kilter. I rarely broke out of habit, and never without notice. He put the back of his hand gently to my forehead. "You don't have a temperature."

"I'm okay, little bit of a headache that's all. I'll get your sandwich," I replied, shaking off his hand and heading over to the refrigerator to grab the sandwich meat.

I loved Daniel. Kind of. He'd been the one to pick me up and put me back together when Joel had gone and his persistence had paid off in the end. I'd gotten used to him being around and I became fond of him.

There was never the kind of heat there that I'd had with Joel though. I guessed it was normal to feel that way after your first love. The butterflies and passion fade and then you're left with what I had with Daniel: stability and affection.

We had our young son, Jacob, and we lived in a nice little house in a good neighbourhood. It was a far cry from the pokey little trailer I'd grown up in. Love or not, I wouldn't let my son grow up as I had with an absent mother and alcoholic father. I was with Daniel for the long haul. I guess that's why he couldn't understand why I kept rejecting his marriage proposals; heck even I didn't understand it. It's not like some knight in shining armour was going to come and carry Jacob and I away to live in a fairy-tale land.

One of these days I was going to have to give in and say yes. God knows I should marry him and get rid of my stupid name; besides, he was a good man and a good father. He had loved me even though he knew deep down I didn't love him in the same way. What was I waiting for?

I took Daniel's sandwich over to the dining table and placed it in front of him with a forced smile. He *was* a good man, so why did the thought of marrying him make me feel sick to my stomach? Apart from Joel he was the only man I'd been with. He had always been good to me and if patience was a virtue then Daniel really was a saint.

In the early days I was a crazy person; black was my signature colour and it definitely matched my mood. I had dyed jet-black hair, thick black eyeliner and mascara; the only shade in my wardrobe besides black was grey. No wonder when Joel and the others left, no one would come near me.

Except for Daniel. Slowly, patiently, he broke down my walls and drew me in to his life, and eventually his social circle. I hated them; all smart ass preppies–everything the guys and I had stood against: perfect hair, smiles, homes and families, not to mention the expanse of money that would no doubt get them into the best schools.

I smiled to myself smugly as I thought how disgusted Joel, Billy and Waz would be at my set up today. I lived in house surrounded by a white picket fence and I was a member of the PTA for Jacob's school... Hell, I was even our old high schools' guidance counsellor!

This was definitely the epitome of everything the four of us said we *didn't* want as adults. Of course I could see now that we were jealous, angry kids brought up on the wrong side of town; dragged up, actually. Our parents had no interest in us and the rest of the town had written us off as trailer trash.

I felt bad for the kids who lived in that trailer park now. My guilt each time I saw one of them traipsing through the halls at school must have radiated off me. I got out; how many of them would be able to say the same by the time they got to my age?

My thoughts were interrupted when I caught sight of Daniel staring at me expectantly.

"Earth to Indiana," he said seriously. "Where were you?"

"Oh just thinking about work, a kid is giving me some trouble." I felt bad for lying but I was a master of it; Daniel never seemed to know when I was doing it.

"Speaking of which, I better head back. Lucky you not having to go five days a week," he smiled and kissed me on the cheek as he made his was out of the house and back to his car.

I waved him goodbye from the front porch like the dutiful little wife I pretended to be, all the while the riot girl inside screamed and raged at my conformity. I gave her a mental pat on the head and she threw herself on the floor of my porch in a tantrum.

"Tell me about it," I said to myself, and shut the front door on her.

"I don't know where your head's at lately Indiana," I cringed as Daniel called me by my full name.

I hated it to the point that it actually made my blood boil. Indiana reminded me of the cosmic joke my parents had made of me from birth. It was worse now that Daniel didn't do it by way of teasing me, but that he actually meant it to scold me.

"Oh, I'm sorry *Daniel*," I replied, my voice dripping with sarcasm. I had only forgotten my car keys–it wasn't the end of the world. We were out on the porch and I knew where I'd left them. "Just unlock the door and I'll grab them, no harm no foul."

He unlocked the door with a huff and I ran inside. Jacob was giggling at his silly mommy; he certainly hadn't inherited his father's straight-laced personality. When I returned to the porch I jingled my keys and Jacob gave me one of his heart-melting smiles. He really was the best thing to have ever happened to me, I thought as my heart swelled with love for him.

"Come on Jakey, let's get outta here!" I ruffled his blonde hair and chased him to the car as Daniel locked up again.

"Jacob!" he called seriously and Jacob's shoulders sagged as he stomped back to his father. Daniel leaned down and pointed to a spot on his cheek for Jacob to kiss. He did so obediently; he hadn't inherited my urges to punch people who did things like that. More so the pity.

Jacob ran back to me and climbed into his booster seat in the front of the car. I closed the door after making sure his seatbelt was buckled properly and made my way round to the driver's side. As I settled into my own seat Jacob looked at me intently.

"Daddy's a real dummy," he said and I stifled a laugh at the serious look on his face.

"That's a mean thing to say Jacob," I half-heartedly scolded him. His daddy *was* a dummy. "Why would you say that?"

"He's no fun, the other kids' daddies laugh and play games," he was so solemn as he spoke that I almost laughed again. He leaned over seriously and whispered, "Shall we run away?"

"Not today kiddo, today we have to go to school," I replied and turned the radio on as I pulled off the drive. Jacob pulled a face at me and we laughed. "Maybe we can run away on Saturday to the lake."

As we neared the end of our street a familiar tune came on the local radio station. I groaned and rolled my eyes. This was happening all too frequently of late.

"Dreaming of coming home to you; talking like we used to do..." I reached to turn off the radio but Jacob pulled my hand away from the dial.

"Stop! I like this one mommy," Jacob smiled at me and drummed his hands on his legs in rhythm with the beat. I forced a smile on my face and gritted my teeth as the song played out.

As the end of the song faded out the radio presenter cut in: "That was 'Coming Home' by our very own local band, The Riots. Rumour has it that Joel, Billy and Waz will really be back in town in coming months! Tune in next week for more news on the boys' return to town."

My breath caught and my stomach lurched–I can't have heard right. My mind went blank as horror pulsed through my body at the news.

"Mommy, mommy!" Jacob's voice cut into the void in my head. I looked down at his terrified face and then out through the windscreen.

We narrowly missed a car coming towards us. I was driving on the wrong side of the road! The other driver blew his horn at us loudly as I swerved out of his way. I pulled on to the grass shoulder and pulled Jacob to me, my heart racing and my head thumping with the start of a headache.

"I'm so sorry baby, I'm so sorry," I was sobbing into his dark blonde hair, hardly believing what I'd just done.

"Mommy you're crazy," he told me as I clung onto him.

They were coming back. Here. Back into our town; my town. And, oh God, I just almost killed my son.

CHAPTER EIGHT

"Mommy, are you sleeping with your eyes open?" Jacob prodded me as I sat staring into my bowl of porridge.

"Huh?" was my bleary-eyed response as I tried to focus on his curious face.

"Excuse me, not huh, mommy." He chastised me. Daniel gave him an approving nod across the table and I fought the urge to punch him in the face. Daniel, not Jacob.

"I'm sorry baby, I have a headache today. What were you saying?" We spent the rest of breakfast listening to Jacob tell us about the naughty kid in his class and how he'd said a bad word and the teacher had sent him to the principle.

I drifted in and out of the conversation. I needed to snap out of this, it was no good for me or for Jacob. Not to mention the fact that Daniel was getting increasingly pissed off with me. No doubt he'd heard the rumour that The Riots were coming to town soon and that paired with me acting like a nut job had him completely rattled.

Jacob finished his breakfast and ran out to the garden to play soccer with our golden Labrador, Bonnie. She was getting old now but loved to race Jacob around the garden and steal the ball away from him.

I cleaned up the dishes and started loading them into the dishwasher, feeling Daniel's eyes on me the whole time. I forced myself to ignore it; I really wasn't in the mood for him this morning.

"It's bothering you that he's coming back," Daniel stood beside me at the kitchen counter. "I know that's why you're acting strangely."

I stopped what I was doing and closed my eyes; I really didn't want to talk about this, not with him. But then with who? I was friendly with the other moms but I had no real friends, just people I passed the time of day with at children's parties and school events.

"Yes, it bothers me. I don't know why. I also don't know why they're coming back here – there's nothing here for any of them." I replied honestly and looked away at the hurt look in Daniel's eyes.

Almost a year after he'd gone, Joel had moved his mom and his sister Casey out of the trailer park and into a fancy house in California. Waz's mom still lived in town but he'd washed his hands of her years earlier; so I'd heard she'd spent all the money he'd sent on drugs and booze and he'd cut her off. There was no reason I could think of that they'd be coming back after all these years.

"It's some MTV thing," Daniel told me and put a print out from the internet on the counter. I looked at him in surprise and he shrugged. "I needed to know why they-why *he*-would come back here."

I scanned the page, avoiding Daniel's gaze; it was a gossip column post about the band and that they'd signed up for an MTV show where they would go back to their hometown and talk about their rags to riches story. That explained it then; another chance to get their mug shots around for all to see.

"Oh, well I guess they shouldn't be around for long then. That's good," I tried to sound dismissive and unbothered by it but my mask must have slipped. Daniel clearly knew me a bit better than I'd given him credit for.

"We could take a vacation? Get out of town for a little bit," he suggested hopefully.

It seemed that the boys' sudden return to town had Daniel as off kilter as I was. He must have felt under threat in some way and wanted us out of town while the band were around.

"Yeah, maybe. We'll see okay." I closed up the dishwasher and threw the print out into the bin as I made my way out to Jacob and Bonnie.

Truth be told, I wanted to be here when they arrived. I wanted to see if Joel had the nerve to look me in the eye. There was something I wanted speak to him about that I was sick of carrying around with me after all of these years.

"Miss Jones, how nice of you to join us." Principle Hardy looked less than impressed with me. Still, I was almost ten minutes late for the faculty meeting so I suppose I could forgive her sarcastic tone.

I took my seat at the long table without a word. I'd had the good grace to grab my notepad and pen from my bag before I entered the room, so as not to cause any further disruption to the meeting. I only worked three days a week, not even full school hours and yet I always managed to get to team meetings by the skin of my teeth. Except today, today I was just plain late. Sleeping with my eyes open again as Jacob had termed it.

I'd decided to Google the band after I dropped Jacob to school and got lost in endless sites spouting gossip about them. I'd just about had enough when I saw the time and had to run, high-heeled, from my office to the other end of the school to the staff meeting room. My feet were screaming at me and my cheeks were flushed from the run; it had been quite a while since I last attempted anything at all like exercise and I made a mental note to use my gym membership more than once a year.

I was rarely called upon to contribute to the staff meetings, I was there more as a nod to the fact I was part of the faculty rather than actually needing to be there. Each department took their turn to debrief the principle on their news and put forward any requests or concerns.

I allowed myself to tune out and mull over what I'd read online about the band. Waz had apparently married a former Playboy bunny girl and I'd giggled to myself when I saw their ridiculously over the top wedding. I also made a mental note to ask him if my invite had gotten lost in the post. From the local gossips I'd gathered that the wedding was reminiscent of Pamela Anderson and Tommy Lee but with the bride dressed in actual clothes-barely.

Billy was a player; as I knew he would be, and he'd been linked with different models, pop stars and actresses almost monthly. Man whore. I could have guessed he hadn't been married; he was too wild to settle down.

And then there was Joel. I'd tried to skip over any romantic links since it made me feel strange but in actual fact he'd hardly been linked to anyone. There was something about him dating an English actress for a while. She was sickeningly photogenic, but other than that he seemed to keep his private life hidden from the gossip columns.

Since hearing they would be back I had looked at recent pictures of them and was surprised to see how much they'd bulked up since I knew them. All three had quite a collection of tattoos; Joel seemed to have the most, with both arms covered from wrists to shoulders.

Waz looked like he'd fallen into the rock star lifestyle of sex and drugs, heavy emphasis on the drugs and I'd seen no pictures of him with the wife I'd been told about. Billy was as handsome as I remembered him, he still had his hair dyed black and wore it spiked and his blue eyes still held the sadness of his trailer park upbringing.

Joel...

"Sorry to interrupt your thoughts Miss Jones but perhaps you'd like to give us your opinion?" Ah damn. Principle Hardy was giving me daggers.

I looked around in utter panic. What did I miss?

"With you having been such good friend with them perhaps you could ask them if they wouldn't mind giving a talk to the students. The Riots I believe they're called?" Rob Shaw looked at me with a smile on his eyes. I loved that man right at that moment for catching me up.

Hang on; he wanted *me* ask them to give a talk? Now I absolutely hated Rob.

"Well, I'm not sure. I can't say I know them at all anymore," I stammered. "They might not even know who I am, you know these rock star types."

"I do believe quite a few of their early hits were written specifically about you and your time together as friends?" I could kick Rob so hard right now. "I'm pretty sure they won't have forgotten you. You're quite the character after all."

Rob was in his mid-thirties and had moved here from another town, but I was fairly sure that if he'd gone to my high school I'd have hated him. Lucky for him my 'character' was quite a bit tamer these days and that I classed him as a friend of sorts.

"Ah Rob, you're quite the character yourself," I replied with a smile through gritted teeth.

CHAPTER NINE

I stepped out of my front porch that Monday morning to find my front yard had been invaded by a stream of reporters and cameramen once more.

Jacob opened his mouth wide and whispered, "Woooowww."

I lifted him up in my arms and hid his face in my shoulder as I pushed through the crowd to get to my car. I had to force the passenger door open, shoving several of them off balance as they fought each other to get close to me. The noise was incredible and the flashes from the cameras surrounding us blinded my eyes.

"Miss Jones have you been in contact with the band regarding their return?" A microphone was shoved in my face as I tried to buckle Jacob into his car seat.

"Please step back, you're upsetting my son," I told them all with a stony faced expression.

The Riots were due to arrive in town the following week and for the last couple of days there had been a media frenzy outside my house. Daniel had taken to working from home as much as possible and was getting increasingly fed up of the attention we were getting. Tensions inside our four walls were rising; we'd not even been able to take the dog for a walk because crazy fans and reporters had quickly descended us upon.

"So have you made plans to meet up with Joel at all Miss Jones?" One reporter pushed herself to the front of the crowd and almost hit me in the face with her mic.

"No comment." I pushed it out of my face and pulled the blanket high over my baby's head before pushing my way through the gaggle of reporters to the driver's side door. "Please leave my property or I'll be forced to call the police."

Daniel had insisted on taking legal advice from his lawyer friend and I repeated what he'd instructed us to say on these occasions. The town was turning into a circus. Someone must have blabbed about my past relationship with Joel because within the first twenty-four hours the media had swept down on me.

They knew where I worked and lived, they knew where Jacob went to school and what class he was in. One tabloid had even gone as far to question who his father was. At which point I thought Daniel might explode. I knew he'd considered taking Jacob out of school and staying with his parents until this whole thing was over.

"It's okay baby, keep that over your face until were down the street," I squeezed his hand then started the car.

The reporters and cameramen stood back to let us pass but I was almost blinded by camera flashes as we passed more on the street outside our house.

"Are you famous mommy?" Came his muffled voice from under the blanket.

"No." I considered how much to tell him, but figured he'd hear all kinds of things from his classmates. "When I was younger I used to be friends with some people who are famous now. I dated one of them for a little while. They're coming to town soon and these people, the reporters, want me to tell them about my old friends."

I pulled the blanket down now we were clear of the cameras. Daniel and I had released a statement saying that we didn't give permission for any images or recordings of Jacob to be used and if they were we would sue. Nonetheless, we'd agreed to hide him as much as we could just in case.

"That's so cool!" He was truly in awe. "When can I meet them? My friends will be so jealous."

"Jakey... I actually think sometimes you're as crazy as your momma." The mind of a small child. If only his father were so relaxed about it all.

I pulled into the high school car lot after dropping Jacob at his school. I wasn't due to start work for a couple of hours but I couldn't stand the thought of fighting through the press to get into the house again. Besides, what was there to go home to? Daniel would just pick a fight as though it was my fault that the vultures had invaded our home.

No, thank you I'd rather be at school. I laughed at the thought. Ten years ago I'd never imagine myself thinking this way.

My laughter quickly turned to tears, what the hell was wrong with me? I was so hormonal and emotional that I could barely think straight. My life had been ticking along just fine and then BOOM, it was like a bomb had gone off and I didn't know left from right anymore.

It was coming to 'that' time of year I realised suddenly. The anniversary.

"Oh my God, what am I doing?" I cried to myself and rested my head on the steering wheel.

Maybe Daniel had been right; we should have taken Jacob and left while the circus was in town. Jacob thought he had a crazy person for a mother at the best of times, he must think I'd completely lost it these past couple of weeks.

There was a sharp knock on the window. *Great.* I wound the window down without moving my head from the wheel.

"Can I help you?" I asked from my hiding place.

"Can you imagine what you must look like to the kids in the classroom over there?" Rob asked mocking me.

"Shit… is there really a class in there?" I tried to peek over the dashboard of my car without showing my face.

"Yup. Now scoot over." I did as I was told and sat up, trying to hide my face behind my loose hair. Thank goodness I'd decided against tying it up this morning.

Rob turned the key and drove us out of the parking lot and headed towards town. I glanced sideways at him; he was handsome in the conventional sense but he didn't have the look that appealed to me. He was too wholesome and 'pretty' for a man with his soft face, plump lips and slender body. He wasn't skinny but he wasn't overly muscular either. I turned my attention back to the road when I realised he'd spotted me watching him.

"Now they'll tell their friends that you were talking to yourself and crying and then I came to take you away," he said matter-of-factly. "And hey presto, we'll be having an affair according to the entire population of the student body."

I groaned loudly; he was right of course. I hit my face with the palm of my hand. Now I was crazy for all to see and apparently having an affair with my colleague. Who I hated, for the record.

"The girls will all hate you of course," he laughed at me, his grey eyes shining with mischief.

"Oh, and why's that then?" I mumbled.

"Because I'm like *so* desirable," he said impersonating a typical teenage girl. "And so they'll totally have to hate you because you have what they want."

"A mental condition?" I said, my voice dripping in sarcasm as I rolled my eyes at him. He looked at me curiously so I continued. "Well I do talk to myself, cry in the car for all to see and not to mention my apparent *terrible* taste in men."

"Ah Indiana, I do love our little talks," Rob pulled into a space outside a small coffee shop that the teaching staff frequented.

It was in the style of an antique bookshop and looked entirely unappealing to teenage eyes. Of course school staff in the town loved it; the coffee was good too but the bonus was definitely that it was a childfree zone.

"I thought you'd appreciate a little grown up time with a mature, sensitive man," Rob smiled and held out his arm for me to take. In spite of myself I hooked my own arm into his and rested my head on his shoulder.

"I'm crazy, aren't I?" I asked.

"Certifiable, baby."

CHAPTER TEN

"So, you used to date one of the guys from the band?" Rob and I were walking through to the lunch hall after that morning's faculty meeting.

"Who told you that?" For a guy who didn't come from this town he sure picked up a lot of old gossip.

"I have my sources," he replied, tapping his nose. "So did he break your teenage heart or did you stamp his into a million pieces?"

The guy was a joker. If I'd had a teacher like him when I was a student here I might have enjoyed history more. I gave him my best evil glare and ignored him.

"He broke your heart then, nasty." Rob laughed and put his arm around my shoulders jovially. "Indiana Jones I'll break you one of these days and all your dirty secrets will come gushing out of that pretty mouth of yours."

"Go fu-." Rob put his hand over my mouth mid-profanity.

"Ah ah ah, students might hear that filth Miss Jones!" He cut me off mid-curse. "So are you looking forward to seeing them? I also heard you'd been great friends with them all but only went out to California once to see them?"

"My God, where do you get your information from!" I was surprised that he knew so much and I had no idea where he'd gotten his information from since I sure as heck never told anyone.

"Yes, we were good friends," I gave in, shaking my head at his pushiness. "There was no reason for me to go back to California, it's not my kind of place. Yes, I dated Joel for a while. Yes, he broke my heart. We were teenagers; don't all teenagers break each other's hearts? It's all part of growing up."

"So you are excited to see them again, him specifically?" He pushed, winking at me jovially.

"I am actually going to beat you to death and bury you in the school basement if you don't mind your own business!" I growled, only partly in jest. Half the time I gave in and told him things only because if you didn't he'd keep asking questions anyway and stare at you with his grey eyes until you felt like your head might spin off. "I doubt I'll see or speak to any of them. We were friends a long time ago, a lot's happened since then."

"You'll see them. I have a feeling about that." Rob smiled and left me in the doorway to the lunch hall open mouthed.

If he said it would happen, it would happen. Most likely because he'd *make* it happen.

I froze at the entrance to the school theatre, my feet rooted to the ground. As usual, when put on the spot, my brain turned to mush. The only clear thought I has was *'Rob, I am going to kill you'*.

"Ah, I did wrong," he whispered guiltily at my side.

"Yeah ya did," I finally managed between gritted teeth. "What were you *thinking*?"

"Revenge? Confrontation?" he tried helplessly.

"What!" I looked at him with raised eyebrows.

"Well, they wanted a scoop and I thought you could dish the dirt on them," Rob blanched at the look on my face. "I got this really wrong."

I stared at him in disbelief, murder in my eyes. "Does my privacy mean *nothing* to you Rob?"

"I thought maybe it was time to confront your past, left to you it would stay buried," he shrugged ruefully.

Laid out on the high school stage in front of us was a set that looked like it had come right out of a daytime chat show. People were mulling around angling cameras and adjusting lighting. Dead set in the middle of it all were two long couches with a presenter perched at the end of the one on the left-hand side.

On the right-hand one sat The Riots, all eyes on me and shifting nervously. The blonde coiffed one followed their gaze and stood up to come and meet me.

"Indiana," she rushed towards Rob and I. "So wonderful to meet you darling."

She then had the audacity to air kiss me on each cheek and grin at me toothily. When I didn't respond except to stare at her like she was an alien, she moved on to Rob.

"Robert, darling, thank you for making this possible!" she kissed both of his cheeks too. "We're *super* excited about this– thank you again for the loan of the theatre."

She clicked her manicured fingers and a young guy seemingly wrapped in wires and wearing a headset appeared at her side obediently.

"Wire her up," she ordered dryly, glancing at her watch and then turning on her sparkling smile for me once more. "Indiana, I'm Betsy and we'll be looking to roll in eight minutes. Don't be shy, just pretend the cameras aren't there."

She was ushering me to the stage as the wireman shoved something rubber into my ear and clipped a miniature microphone to my blouse.

"Hey buster!" I exclaimed as he began to tuck his hand inside my blouse to secure the mic. "Move it or lose it."

He looked mortified but I was furious about being man handled. He carefully took his hand out of my top and held it up and rushed away from me, backwards. Next a woman with caramel skin and big red lips appeared and started powdering my face with a huge make up brush. I put my hand out to stop her for a moment.

"I didn't agree to any of this," I fumed, twisting around to glare at Rob. He was now seated in the front row of the theatre, immediately behind the lighting set up.

Betsy's jaw dropped. "But you're the focal point of this section Indiana."

"Focal point–section? What are you talking about?" I snapped at the stupid, annoying Betsy.

"The 'memory lane' part of the documentary we're making sweetie," she replied patiently, as though speaking to a small child. "We're going to speak to you about the origins of the band; a kind of 'before they were famous exposé if you will."

I looked at Rob again and gave him a death stare as Betsy continued to push me on stage, waving the make-up girl away. I couldn't bring myself to so much as glance in the direction of the boys on the other sofa; I was torn between kicking their asses and running away.

Taking a deep breath, I tried to regain my composure. My heart was racing and I was a wreck. There was no use denying it. But I was a grown up now, a mother for goodness sake–I could handle this.

Except for Rob, I thought, *he was a dead man walking.*

Closing my eyes for a moment I took another breath before forcing myself to look in the direction of the other couch. For the first time in almost seven years I was looking at them in the flesh once more.

Waz looked shocking, his eyes were drawn with dark circles underneath, and he looked like he needed a good home-cooked meal. Billy waved his hand at me with a nervous smile. *Good*, I thought, *so he should be nervous.* He was still handsome but with more ink on his skin than I remembered.

Joel stared at me intently, drinking me in. I felt sick to my stomach.

"So, Indiana, tell us about the guys you knew and loved growing up," the bottle blonde airhead with bright red lips known as Betsy began. Her hair was like a helmet, it had been sprayed to within an inch of its life and I was mesmerised by it.

"Oh well I didn't really know them all that well back then," I lied.

The boys looked at me with confusion; but I had decided that the sooner I got out of there, the better – if Betsy thought I didn't know them then she'd surely cut the interview immediately.

"Now don't be so coy *Indiana*," God I hated her for using my full name. "I have video tapes from your old days in the band! You were their original 'fourth' so they tell me. How did it feel when you got cut from the band?"

I glared at her. *What a bitch*, I thought.

"In actual fact I left the band of my own volition. I quit before the scout even noticed them. The band being famous that was always their dream and I was just dragged along as a vocalist for a while," I told her straight. "I was there the night the scout picked them up and I was–and am–happy for them. I'm proud of what they've achieved."

"Can you tell us what they were like before the fame?" Betsy pushed.

"They were my best friends," I confessed. "The only real family I had around. They were funny and kind and everything a friend should be."

I looked at each of them in turn, looking them right in the eye. A tear slipped down my cheek and I glanced away quickly, wiping it with the back of my hand.

"How did you feel when they were signed?" Betsy smiled. "It must have been exciting to think you knew them before they were famous?"

"Actually I was over the moon for them," I leant in conspiratorially. "Because I'd helped write some of their earlier songs, they were good enough to send me a few checks from those first couple of albums. So, as I'm sure you can imagine, I was delighted when they got signed and started to make it big. Who needs friends around when you have checks rolling in?"

Joel closed his eyes and pinched his nose. I wondered what was going through his mind. Did he understand what I had really meant in my thinly veiled comment?

"And..." Betsy was struggling now; she really hadn't expected that little titbit of information. "What did you do with the money?"

"I put myself through college and brought the house I live in now," I replied without skipping a beat. "In short, I support myself and my *son* with that money. The guys will tell you, growing up the way we did, you learn not to depend on anyone but yourself. That money made sure I never had to rely on anyone else. And that's why you won't hear a bad word about a single one of them from me; they could easily have cut me out but they didn't. They made sure I was taken care of and paid for the part I played in the band until that point. Now, if you'll excuse me I have to fetch my son."

Joel looked up in surprise at the mention of Jacob he hadn't been expecting that. Perhaps he thought I'd sat alone and pined for him all this time without building a life of my own.

I hadn't told anyone about the royalty checks until then. Little did I know, that day after I'd left my Dad's trailer for the last time, I was carrying in my pocket the first of several royalty checks. There was a short note inside–*For you, Indi.* That was all the contact I had from them.

Only the bank had any idea about the extra cash that came into my account and where it had come from. As I marched out of the room I realised I had been mad long enough. It was time to face him one to one.

CHAPTER ELEVEN

I was surprised to find Daniel was home early when I came in. One look at him meant one thing: I was in trouble.

"Jakey honey, why don't you take Bonnie outside to play, she's been cooped up all day," I smiled at him, ushering him and Bonnie out of the patio doors.

"Jesus Christ, Indiana–the whole fricking town is talking about your interview today! Why the hell didn't you tell me?" Daniel paced the kitchen, throwing his hands in the air as he ranted.

Apparently the gossips had sources better than my own, the rest of the world seemed to know my business before I did recently.

"It was as much of a surprise to me as it was to you, trust me. I was set up by a so-called friend." I slumped down into a chair and put my head down on the dining table.

The cold surface felt good on my forehead, soothing my busy brain. I lifted my head and watched Jacob running around the yard, Bonnie hot on his heels as he giggled away. That smile of his melted my heart; he was beginning to look so much like Joel now...

"You're going to tell him, aren't you?" Daniel's face contorted in pain as he followed my gaze out of the open patio doors.

"I honestly haven't decided," I rested my head in my hands, pushing my hair back. "Part of me thinks he *should* know, and then I remind myself that Joel is–ridiculously–a rock star with a crazy life and I don't want Jacob affected by that. Besides–*you* are Jacob's father."

"I knew this day would come," Daniel's eyes filled with tears. "Please don't take him away from me Indi."

"Never," I stood up and held him, hiding my face in his neck and breathing in the scent of him. "Never, Daniel."

Rob owed me big time, and I called in his debt by getting him to arrange for me to see Joel alone and 'off the record'. He'd had to go through Betsy–he'd clearly managed to charm her, though how I didn't wish to know.

I felt guilty about sneaking off to meet him behind Daniel's back, but he wouldn't approve of me seeing Joel. He was feeling incredibly insecure and he was at the end of his tether with the press camping out in our front yard.

Joel and I had opted for a coffee shop just outside town. We agreed to meet in the early morning in hopes that no one would be around to recognise him or photograph us. I decided to take Bonnie as an alibi; it wasn't unusual for me to take her on an early morning jog with me so my absence wouldn't cause suspicion.

I sat in my car, nervously biting at my nails as Bonnie panted warm dog breath in my face. I patted her head gently as I contemplated leaving.

"What am I doing, Bon-Bon?" I asked her. "I'm such a damn idiot."

There was a tap on my window, causing me to start and my hand flew to my chest. It was Joel. My heart raced, whether from the fright or the sight of his face so close to my own, only the glass separating us. He was still as handsome as ever, his eyes piercing me.

I fumbled with the door handle and stepped out of the car, Bonnie jumping out beside me with her golden tail wagging happily. Joel knelt down to greet her.

"Hey beautiful," he said as she nuzzled his hand excitedly.

"Sorry. She's my, well, she's my alibi I guess," I shrugged nervously as he stood back up.

Being nervous around Joel was a whole new experience for me. My heart felt like it might burst out of my chest, and my hands were clammy–I wiped my palms hastily on my sweatpants; I'd even dressed as though I was going for a jog. I couldn't quite bring myself to look him in the eye.

"Alibi?" he looked amused. "Well let's take her for a walk then, shall we."

"Come on Bon-Bon," I called her to heel and she obediently trotted by my side. "I'm with someone you see, he wouldn't be happy if he knew I was here, with you. So I brought Bonnie with me so he wouldn't be suspicious. We've had reporters following us lately, he's not too happy."

"I'm sorry about that, hazard of the job for me but it's not fair that they're bugging you," he said apologetically. "Who is he? Someone from town?"

"His name is Daniel–you probably wouldn't remember him, but he was in our class at school," I replied, trying to sound relaxed. "We live in a little house just out of the main town."

"With your kid…" he finished.

"Yeah, my son–Jacob," I felt myself tense up as the subject came to Jacob. "He's a great kid."

"Are you happy?" he asked.

We found a bench and sat down; I unclipped Bonnie's leash and threw her ball for her. Joel's question had taken me by surprise; *was* I happy? I had a good job–one that I didn't hate at least; a son I adored and a nice home. And a stable, normal relationship.

"Yeah, I guess I am happy. I don't want for anything and I have a good life," I answered, and then smiled. "Obviously I'm not a rich, famous rock star but you can't have everything, right?"

He chuckled at that comment. "It's not all it's cracked up to be."

We sat in silence for a while, both of us watching Bonnie as she tossed her ball up into the air and chased her tail in circles. Joel broke the silence first.

"I missed you Indi…"

"Don't," I cut him off, aware of the anger starting to bubble up inside of me. "Please, just don't."

I wiped a tear away, caused more by the anger and pain than the sadness. He put his hand on mine and I pulled it away.

"I'm sorry," he tried again.

"So, are you happy?" I turned the question on him.

He took a deep breath. "No, not really. I'm exhausted, and lost."

I was surprised by his response. I turned to look at him properly for the first time, daring to take him in. He did look exhausted, there were dark circles under his eyes and the smile, which I had always known to play on the corners of his mouth, was gone, replaced by the frown lines on his forehead. I could see that his answer had been genuine.

"What happened to you?" I asked quietly.

"I left you," he returned my gaze.

Without even realising I had done it, I found myself holding his face in the palms of my hands and I kissed him softly. His lips felt soft and warm on my own as they brushed together.

"You did," I replied and stood up to leave, whistling for Bonnie to come to me.

Joel grabbed hold of my hand. "Don't go."

"I have to Joel," I answered, pulling my hand away and clipping Bonnie's leash back on to her collar. "I have to get back for Jacob."

"Can I see you again?" his eyes pleaded with me.

"Yes." I walked away quickly, before I lost myself in him once more.

It was a few days later that I got a text from Joel, asking to meet up in the same place again. Daniel was at work and Jacob was at school so I agreed to go along.

When I got to the park Joel was sat on the ground, running the grass through his hands with a faraway look on his face. I stood and watched him for a moment, taking him in. Age hadn't changed him; he still had the ability to give me butterflies and bring to the surface all the feelings I had buried deep inside for the past seven years.

"Hey," I called out, as I got nearer.

Joel looked up, beamed at me and then indicated for me to join him on the grass. "It's nice here, so quiet. I'd forgotten what it was like to just sit and be quiet for a while."

"I guess between gigs, recording and screaming fans you don't get a lot of quiet time?" I smiled.

"You can say that again," he nodded. "Sitting outside alone is almost impossible, there's always someone asking for a picture or an autograph. Though it's not as bad now as it was a couple of years ago. That's why our manager wanted us to do this show—he thinks it'll push us back into the limelight, give people some fresh interest in us."

"Getting to be old news, huh?" I pulled at the grass, spreading my fingers to let the blades fall back to the ground. "Younger, prettier rock stars starting to take your place?"

"Something like that," he laughed. "No dog today?"

"Nah, though she wasn't impressed about being left," I replied. "Daniel's at work today and Jake's at school so I didn't have to make up an excuse to come out."

"I found my old yearbook," he said, looking at the ground sheepishly. "I remember him now. I gotta admit I'm more than a little shocked that you're with that... that-*guy*."

I had a rough idea about what he really wanted to call Daniel but the look on my face clearly put him off letting the words leave his mouth.

"You don't understand," I replied, fighting back tears. "You don't know what he did for me when you left. I was completely alone here."

"So how long was it after I'd gone that you jumped his bones?" He was getting angry now and his words made me see red.

"You hypocritical son of a bitch!" I rounded on him; fighting the urge to hit him, I shoved him instead. "You left me! I came to find you and was told there was no place for me in your life anymore and to stay away!"

Tears stung my eyes as I kept pushing him until he fell back against the ground, taking me with him. He'd had hold of my arm and I fell on top of him, before quickly scrambling away. I pulled my knees up to my chest protecting myself against the torrent of emotions.

"I came to tell you..." The sobs overwhelmed me now, bringing back pain I'd buried inside for almost seven years. "I–I..."

"For God's sake, what Indi?" He was looking at me like I was losing my mind. Maybe I was.

My legs sagged down; I was completely spent and resigned to my fate. I whispered my response.

"What? I can't hear a word you're saying," he pulled my chin upwards so he could look at me properly.

"I was pregnant," I cried. "We had a baby."

He sank down beside me. His turn to be shocked and crazy. "What... How... Where is it?"

I sucked in a deep breath, blowing my cheeks out and pushed the air back out. Joel put his arm around me and I didn't have the strength to fight him off so I let him sit there and comfort me like he should have done years earlier, as I watched our son grow inside me.

When I recovered enough to speak I straightened myself out and rubbed my smudged mascara away with the back of my hand.

"I got the bus to see you in California. When I got there some guy called Paulie gave me a roll of money and told me to 'take care of it'," the words came tumbling out, as though a dam had broken. "Dad kicked me out when he found out. Daniel pretended to be the father and so his parents very generously gave us somewhere to live."

"I'm so sorry, you have to believe me, I just didn't know." Joel had tears running down his face and for the briefest moment I was seventeen and in love with him again.

Was I ever out of love with him? I wondered. No, there was too much water under the bridge for me to think this way.

"He came too early," I continued. "He was so tiny. We spent weeks in the hospital waiting for him to be strong enough to come home. I tried to contact you again but the record company wouldn't let me speak to you. Your mum and Darcy had left already. I wanted you to see him."

"What happened to him?" He reached for my hand but I moved out of his grasp, just as he had moved from mine all those years ago.

"Jacob…" I whispered.

Joel's jaw dropped open before he burst into a huge smile. "Jacob, he-he's mine?"

"Yeah," I nodded. Words failed me now. "Shit, I have to go."

I stood up and brushed my clothes down with my hands. I'd have to fix my face in the car before Jacob saw me.

"Can I-can I come with you?" Joel looked at me awkwardly as he stood up beside me. "I'd like to meet him."

I paused to consider his request. He looked so broken and I pitied him for the turmoil he now had to deal with. But Jacob was not a pawn in this game.

"No, not today. I have to speak to Daniel first. Maybe another time," I replied. I smiled as I thought of his inquisitive little face. "He'd like to meet you though, he thinks this media circus is the best thing since Teenage Mutant Ninja Turtles. He doesn't know though, and I don't want him to-not yet."

"Why not?" Joel asked, without any malice.

"I'm not sure if he should know at all," I replied honestly. "Daniel is the only father he's known, your life is too crazy for him to have a place in. I want him to have the stability we never had as kids. I want him to be normal and to fit in. We never did and if he knows who you really are then he will never be normal again."

Joel looked like he might argue, but then thought better of it and nodded sadly. "Okay."

When he got home that evening I surprised Daniel with his favourite meal: spaghetti with meatballs. I'd given Jacob his dinner early and had put him to bed, where he was happily watching TMNT on his TV.

"To what do I owe this pleasure?" he smiled as I took his jacket from him and hung it up.

I poured us both a glass of wine as I served dinner up. Daniel looked bewildered; admittedly, this it was out of character for me to be the doting housewife lately. He usually came home to Jacob's toys all over the living room floor and me guiltily offering to get take-out since I'd forgotten the time and hadn't gotten dinner ready.

"Let's do it," I said, much to Daniel's surprise. "Let's get married. I don't know why it's taken me so long but let's get married. As soon as possible."

"I don't know Indi, are you sure about this?" Daniel practically fell into the chair and gulped back his wine. I thought that he might be in shock or something.

"Yes. One hundred percent sure, let's do it!" My inner cheerleader was doing a little victory dance while the riot girl threw herself on the floor in her usual tantrum.

I tried to ignore them both as I concentrated on staying in the here and now. *That's important,* I thought to myself; if my mind wondered again then Daniel would definitely say no.

"I always thought if I asked enough times then one day you'd give in," he said to the room in general. "I just never really thought it would actually work."

He looked... unnerved I suppose was the word I was looking for. I suddenly felt uneasy. After asking me at least a dozen times it was starting to look like perhaps this wasn't what he'd wanted. I felt a little deflated and hurt at his reaction.

"I think perhaps we should sleep on this, Indi," he kissed me on the forehead as my face fell. "Everything has been so nuts lately, I think it would be better to have a think on it. Let's make sure this is what you really want, okay?"

"Okay," I nodded and forced a smile.

CHAPTER TWELVE

I opened my front door the next day to find Billy's smiling face waiting on my porch. He gave me a huge hug, sweeping me up and spinning me around.

"Baby, you look amazing," he told me as he kissed my cheek. "I missed you!"

"Missed me so much you forgot to send me that bus ticket, huh?" I teased.

"We never meant to leave you behind, Indi," Billy looked at me sadly. "The whole thing kind of ran away with us, but you must believe that we never forgot you–especially Joel…"

"I guess that it's all just water under the bridge now," I shrugged even though I did still feel I was owed a proper explanation. "Hey, do you like the house you guys paid for?"

I turned and waved my hands with flair at my redbrick, one-storey home. I was sure it was nothing compared to the kind of house he must own but I was still proud of my little piece of the world.

"It was *your* money, you earned it," Billy pointed out. "Very nice Ind; although kinda low key for you. I'd have pictured blacked out windows and a goth'ed up front yard with black and purple plants!"

"Well, I tried but the neighbours complained–what's a girl to do?" I winked. "So, do you want to come in?"

"Yes ma'am," he curtsied and laughed as I let him in.

I remembered a spilt-second too late that Jacob was inside eating lunch, and Billy was bound to know about him by now. I just hoped he hadn't lost any of his tact and kept him mouth shut about Joel in front of my son.

"Wow! Mom, that's the guy from TV," Jacob spotted Billy right away, pointing at him as he jumped down from the table.

"Finish your lunch please Jacob," I told him sternly and guided him back to the table, rolling my eyes to Billy. "It's rude to point Jacob. Please excuse my son, he was born with ants in his pants."

Jacob giggled and sat back down, staring at Billy wide-eyed the whole time. Billy leant down next to Jacob and held his hand out.

"Nice to meet you Jacob, my name's Billy," he and Jacob shook hands with a smile.

"Nice to meet you too," Jacob replied politely. "What are you doing at our house mister?"

Billy laughed. "Your mom and I were good friends when I was your age and so I just wanted to come over and say 'hi'."

Jacob looked at me questioningly and I nodded. "Remember, I told you about the boys from that band on the radio? Billy was like a brother to me."

"Cool," Jacob said between mouthfuls of ham sandwich and then turned his attention back to Billy. "Wanna watch TMNT with me Billy?"

Billy looked at me for an explanation; clearly he was not 'down with the kids' like me.

"Teenage Mutant Ninja Turtles to you and I," I explained. "Sorry Jakey, not today."

Jacob looked disappointed but didn't argue; I was grateful that he wasn't a whiney kid like some of his classmates at school. I couldn't help but wonder what Billy made of his newfound nephew.

"Take Bonnie with you to the lounge when you're finished buddy. Billy and I are going to catch up outside," I told him, heading over to the refrigerator.

I grabbed a beer for Billy and poured myself a glass of juice. Though, if not for Jacob, I'd have gladly gotten a beer for myself. I led Billy out through the patio doors into the backyard, setting myself down in the swing chair.

"I thought I was going to have to fight my way through a bunch of reporters. Joel said you'd had trouble with them?" Billy asked.

I smiled coyly to myself. I'd had enough this morning and had played a little prank.

"Well, you see I heard that they had an anonymous tip-off that you guy's might be over at some guy called Rob's place over the next couple of days."

"Rob... That guy from the school theatre?" Billy replied. "Isn't he a friend of yours?"

"Uh huh," I beamed mischievously. "I figured he wouldn't mind a little pay-back, he does enjoy a good prank."

"Ahh, I get it now–still a little fire cracker then Miss Jones?" Billy chuckled.

"I still have my moments." I sipped my juice and turned to watch Jacob put his plate in the dishwasher before padding out to the living room with Bonnie at his heel.

"Joel told me," Billy followed my gaze then looked at me earnestly. "He's a beautiful kid, Indi."

"I tried to tell him, you know. I desperately needed him–all of you really–when I found out I was pregnant," I looked into my glass of juice, a lump in my throat. "I missed you all so much."

Billy put him arm around my shoulders and I rested my head on him. It felt like the years melted away. Billy was still just the kid from a couple of trailers back–my confidant, one of my closest friends, not some famous guy from the TV and radio. A tear slipped down my cheek, but I didn't attempt to wipe it away.

"You won't believe it, not with all that's happened, but we really missed you. Whenever your name came up, we all felt so bad about you being back here and not there with us," he kissed the top of my head.

"Why didn't you come back for me?" I cried softly. "You promised you wouldn't leave me here."

"We kept getting told 'maybe later', and we were so scared that the label would ship us back home if we did something wrong that we didn't push as hard as we should've," he explained.

He held me tight in his tattooed arms and I traced one of the pictures with my fingertip as I listened to his familiar voice.

"Can I be honest though?" he asked and I nodded. "Don't take this the wrong way, but I'm glad you didn't come."

I tensed up at his confession. Billy and I had been so close once, why hadn't he wanted me there? I looked up at him accusingly.

"Back in your cage Indi," he winked and pulled me back to him. "We changed a lot in those early days, we tried to please all these assholes and frankly I'm ashamed of us. I'm glad you didn't get to see all of that; you'd have hated us. God, you'd have killed us for some of the stuff we agreed to, acting like sheep."

"Maybe you needed a good ass-kicking?" I smiled to myself. "It took until Jacob was born to finally give up hope of you ever sending for me. He was born early–I almost lost him, I realised then that I had to just let you all go. That I had to let Joel go."

"He's still in love with you," Billy's words caused the tears to flow freely.

The next day Billy was at my doorstep once more, this time I was home alone since Daniel had taken Jacob over to see his brother across town for a few hours.

"I hear the paps got a tip-off about that Rob guy again," Billy pointed to the empty front yard with a smile. "I wanted to bring you to see Waz–he needs an ass-kicking that only you can give."

I grabbed my keys and followed Billy out to his blacked out jeep. "Is he okay?"

"Not really, you probably noticed that he looks like shit, right?" Billy said as we pulled away from my house. "I know we promised Indi but he is a force of nature; he's been messing with all kinds of drugs over the last few years."

I was furious. "What an idiot! I thought he looked terrible when I saw him last week, I should have guessed."

Reaching over, I punched Billy hard in the arm.

"Ow, what was that for?" I whined.

"For breaking your promise to me, you said you'd make sure he was okay. I *knew* this would happen."

Ten minutes later we pulled into their hotel parking lot and made our way up to Waz's suite. Billy banged on the door a couple of times but Waz didn't answer.

"I have a swipe card here somewhere," Billy patted down his leather jacket and eventually pulled out a white plastic card and waved it against the door pad.

The door clicked and we pushed it open. The room was a mess, towels and clothes and junk all over the floors and chairs. It took me a moment to register the figure on the king-sized bed across the room.

"Waz, wake up!" I watched, horrified as Billy rushed over to shake Waz's lifeless body, surrounded by needles and other drug paraphernalia.

Vomit covered his chin and was pooled on the sheets next to his head. There was a strange silence as I stood watching the scene in front of me; it was as though the earth had come to a standstill and all that was left moving was Billy and I.

I snapped to as I heard Billy calling my name and the world swooped in on us once more.

"Indi! I said call for an ambulance!" he shouted at me.

I clumsily pulled my cell phone from my jeans pocket and dialled 911. "I-I need an ambulance."

Suddenly time was on fast forward and before I knew it Waz was rushed away from us and we were sitting in the sterile hospital waiting room.

"How the hell did his habit get this bad?" I paced the tiled floor, half angry and the other half just plain terrified for my old friend. "You promised me!"

Billy sat on the red plastic chair with his head cupped in his tattooed hands and watching my feet as I moved back and forth in front of him. People in the waiting room were watching us with interest – a couple of them had even gotten their phones out to photograph us: the rock star and the crazy chick.

"I don't know Ind, it's crazy out there. It's not like anything else you've ever known..." Billy tried to explain.

"The circus that follows you guys everywhere will be all over this soon Billy," I threw myself down on the chair next to him and ducked my head down as more people started to watch and photograph us. "Are there people you should call?"

Billy eyed the growing crowd and groaned. "Shit, yeah, I gotta call our manager, he'll get someone down here. We should get out of this place and find out what's happening with Waz."

CHAPTER THIRTEEN

Waz was already dead when we found him. That much I understood through the chaos in my head. I had been photographed by the journalists going into, and then leaving, the hospital that day and Daniel was beyond angry.

Still he'd left me alone to deal with my grief, which is all I could ask for. Waz and I hadn't seen or spoken to each other in seven years but the sorrow I felt was as raw as if I'd spoken to him just yesterday. The image of him lying on the bed in his own vomit would never leave me.

I'd taken Jacob and Bonnie to the park to try and clear my head. Billy and I had spoken briefly on the phone and I knew that the record company were keeping him and Joel busy with band business over the few days, which followed Waz's death.

I was surprised to look up and find Joel making his way over to my spot on the grass. It was the spot where he and I had lay together with Billy and Waz years before, when our relationship was brand new and shiny.

I stood up to greet him, holding each other tightly in silence. Stepping back I took his face in my hands to look at him; his eyes were red-rimmed and he looked tired. I pulled him back to me and kissed his neck, wanting so much to kiss his soft mouth instead but aware of Jacob's presence.

"Forgive me Indi," he whispered, his warm breath tickling my neck and sending a heat through my body. "Be with me, please."

"I can't live like this Joel, not with the press watching my every move." I looked into his eyes and stepped away from him, hugging myself tightly. "We live in two very different worlds now; this isn't what I want for myself, or for Jacob."

I sat down on the grassy field and watched Jacob playing ball with Bonnie in the distance.

"I have to think of Jacob," I smiled at him sadly. "I wonder all the time what it would have been like if you'd been here to be his daddy."

Joel sat down next to me and locked his hand around my own. I squeezed it gently.

"We would have been a great family; I'd have done anything for you both," he never took his eyes off Jacob as he spoke.

"I feel like this is goodbye," I cupped my other hand over his and held him tightly, fighting the lump in my throat.

"So do I," his voice broke and I looked up to find tears running down his face. "I'm so sorry I left you behind–I, I didn't know."

"What didn't you know?" I asked gently. If this was truly goodbye then I wanted for there to be nothing left unsaid this time around.

"That you would be the thing I regretted most of all," he replied. "At the time everyone was filling our heads with all of this junk; about how we'd be able to do whatever–*who* ever–we wanted. They said we had to leave our old lives behind, that they'd just drag us back. They told us that if we didn't cut off the 'baggage' then we might as well go home and call it quits."

"I was the baggage?" It was my turn to cry. I'd spent so much of my adult life being angry and trying to have him–all of them, really. Now I just wanted to listen to him and try to put myself in their position as I heard what had happened out there.

"That's what they told us everyone from back home was, that they wouldn't understand and they'd try to hold us back. I wanted to see you, to talk to you – I was so confused. But they kept us busy all day with the recording and interviews and stuff and then they'd take us straight from there to party after party." He was staring off into the distance, reliving those first weeks and months as he spoke. "Before long I didn't even know what day of the week it was anymore."

"And Simone?" I asked tentatively. Simone was the only woman I'd found he'd been in a relationship when I looked into him and the others what felt like forever ago.

He looked at me, surprised, and gave a playful laugh. "Google?"

"Uh huh," I admitted shyly.

"The guys from the label kept on at me about 'making the most' of getting famous. That rock stars should be seen out with models and actresses hanging on their arms," Joel looked uncomfortable as he spoke. "Billy got into it, you know?"

"I know," I raised an eyebrow as I recalled the endless list of women I'd seen linked to him in the online gossip sites.

"I wasn't interested in any of that–back here I'd found it funny when all those girls threw themselves at us after a gig," he looked at me seriously. "But that we before you and I got together; before I knew what it was like to lie in bed with a girl who was my best friend *and* girlfriend. The chicks out there in LA are crazy."

"Simone was different?" I was determined to know about her.

"In some ways I guess; she wasn't as loud and obnoxious as the others at any rate. They wanted to be with bad boy rock stars like we were fashion accessories but she wasn't like that. I got with her because I *had* to been seen with a girl, do you understand?"

I shook my head, I didn't understand. "You had to be *seen* with her?"

He shifted uncomfortably and wouldn't meet my gaze.

"Joel?" I pushed him.

He ran his free hand through his dyed black hair. "Ah shit. They started asking if I was *gay*," he whispered the word, looking mortified.

He looked so serious about his 'confession' that I couldn't help myself and burst out laughing hysterically. He bumped my shoulder and I swayed to the side.

"It's not funny dude!" he smiled in spite of himself.

My laughter was contagious and before long we were crying and breathless, propping each other up. Curious, Jacob came running over to us, Bonnie hot on his heels.

"Have you lost it again mommy?" he asked with his head angled to one side and he watched me try to pull myself together.

His seriousness set us both off again and he rolled his eyes at us impatiently.

"Come on Bonnie," he said to the dog. "Mom's crazy is 'tageous, we might get it too."

Joel and I watched the two of them run back to their game and we slowly regained control of ourselves.

"I missed you," I admitted. "I missed us. I can't believe Waz is gone, that you guys will be leaving soon. "

He pulled me close and held me in a tight embrace.

"I don't know if I can leave you again Indi," he spoke softly in my ear, his warm breath giving me goose bumps as it touched my skin.

I breathed him in; he was intoxicating. So many 'what ifs' spun around inside my mind – 'if it was just me'… But it wasn't just me, there was Jacob and he was my entire world. I placed my hands on Joel's face and looked deep into his familiar eyes, pulling him into a kiss.

I put all of the love, loss and pain I'd felt for and over him into that kiss.

Then I stood up and walked away from him.

CHAPTER FOURTEEN

On the way home I dropped Jacob off at one of his friend's houses. Tom's mother had been surprised to see me standing on her doorstep but had said it was okay for him to play for a while.

"I'm sorry to have heard about your friend," she'd said as I turned to leave.

Now I was home and I knew, that even though I couldn't be with Joel that I *shouldn't* be with Daniel either. I had always known, really.

"Where's Jacob?" he looked up from his paper and spotted that only Bonnie and I had come home.

"I dropped him at Tom's house," I explained. "I needed to speak to you and it isn't a conversation I want him to hear."

"You're going back to that jackass, aren't you?" he accused, his face turning red with anger.

"No, no I'm not going back to Joel. He knows that isn't an option," I replied wearily and took a seat next to Daniel. "But I also realise that I can't be with you anymore either, we have to face facts Daniel."

"If you think I'm just going to let you just take my son away…" Daniel stated angrily.

"I'm not taking Jacob anywhere Daniel," I cut him off. "He's your son and I wouldn't do that to either one of you. We're going to stay here, in *my* house, but you can't be here anymore."

He looked furious, but it was too bad because I had made my mind up.

"I don't love you Daniel, you always knew that. You wanted to 'fix' me or something, but if you're honest, you never loved me either. I know how much you do love Jacob, and you will always be his father. Joel knows the truth now, but he agrees–kind of at least–that Jacob shouldn't know about it yet."

Daniel put his head in his hands, perched at the edge of his seat like a bird about to take off. Neither of us spoke for a few moments. I stood up and leant against the kitchen counter in front of him, I felt like I'd said all I needed to.

"I tried," he said finally. "I wanted so much for you to love me. In the beginning I was infatuated with you. You were wild and not afraid of anything while I was the opposite–I was too afraid to be different. You didn't seem to care what anyone thought of you and I wanted you so much."

"I disappointed you once you got me?" I prompted him.

"No–not at all! When I found out you were pregnant I wanted to help you," he spoke softly now, as he always did when talking about Jacob. "I wanted to stand out from the crowd with you; I thought maybe I could catch you and keep you."

Inwardly I was outraged at his confession that he'd knowingly come to me when I was at my most vulnerable, not to help me but to catch me and parade me as some kind of trophy. I bit my tongue, hard– fighting would get us nowhere.

"I was surprised how easily everyone believed he was my baby; how easy it was to convince you to go along with it all," he looked up at me accusingly.

"I was desperate Daniel! I don't mean it in that way, but I was in such a bad place. I had no one, I was devastated that Joel and the others had abandoned me, and there you were, telling me we could say the baby was yours and that everything would be okay." I joined him at the table my head was throbbing.

"We did the wrong thing," he said to the room in general.

"No." I surprised myself with the force of the word. "No–without that decision back then there would be no Jacob. There might not even be *me* anymore if not for you."

I recalled how much of a dark place I'd been in with no one to pull me out of it. I was ashamed to remember the things I'd considered while I felt so alone and had no one to talk to.

"You've been like a caged animal for all of these years Indi," he put his hand on mine and I fought the urge to pull it away. "The only time I see you truly happy is with Jacob."

"He's my life–the sun and the moon to me," I said simply. "I'll always be thankful to you for helping me to keep him."

"He hates me…" Daniel looked crushed.

"No he doesn't," I said earnestly. "He just doesn't understand you; he's almost seven years old and he just wants to have fun with you but you're so serious all of the time. He finds that intimidating and confusing."

"He's so much like you – so curious about the world and unafraid to be different," Daniel smiled sadly.

"He's crazy, I agree," I smiled.

He pulled his hand away from me and stood up, pushing the chair against the wooden floor.

"I'll leave before Jacob comes home, so he doesn't get too upset," I was surprised to hear Daniel give in.

"I'll stay with my brother until I can get somewhere close by with a spare room for Jacob to have when he stays over," Daniel said. "I want more than anything to carry on being his father."

"You've thought of leaving me before now," I realised out loud.

"Yes," he replied simply.

"So it's just you and me now?" Jacob asked, taking in what I'd said.

We were curled up under a fleece blanket on the sofa. I'd gotten us a pizza and we were watching Teenage Mutant Ninja Turtles for the hundredth time, the kid was obsessed.

"Yes, is that okay?" I asked. "I mean, you'll still see your dad all of the time, he just won't live here with us anymore."

"Yeah – I guess," he was thoughtful as he slowly chewed his mouthful of pizza.

"Something you want to ask me Jakey?" I kissed his forehead.

"What if you forget my cereal or burn dinner or forget soccer practice?" he asked and I smiled, hugging him close.

"I'll try not to do any of those things anymore baby. And once daddy gets a place of his own you'll have a second home – you can stay there as much or as little as you want to." I kissed the top of his head and ran my hand over his soft brown hair.

He let out a big yawn and snuggled into me.

"Come on buster, bed for you." I scooped him up into my arms and carried him to his room. "You got so big."

Jacob giggled sleepily as I changed him into his PJs and tucked him up in bed. Bonnie had snuck in behind us and jumped up onto the bed to curl up at his feet. I gave her a look and she wagged her tail, challenging me to move her.

"You win," I whispered and patted her on the head.

As I made my way back to the lounge a glanced towards to the front door. There was a small, flat package on the ground. I scooped it up off the floor and looked for a label or note on the brown paper wrapping but there was nothing. I peeled open the paper and found a CD case with 'play me' written in black marker across the shiny surface.

I placed the silver disc into the CD player and sat on the sofa to listen to it. On the disc was an acoustic album of love songs, words that Joel couldn't say to me during all of our years apart and sung by three boys from my childhood.

I listened to every word, shared every memory they recorded on the CD. By the time the last song ended my face was soaked with tears. I knew then that he was always with me and that he kept a part of me with him too. And now he was gone once more.

I was glad I had made the decision not to tell Jacob the truth about Joel, not just yet anyway. I didn't want Jacob to feel the same sense of loss and heartbreak as I was feeling.

Part Three

Indi, Aged Thirty

CHAPTER FIFTEEN

As I stood in the airport arrivals I could barely contain my excitement. Daniel had moved out of state for work a couple of years earlier. So we had agreed that Jacob would spend the summers with him and the rest of the year with me. Letting my almost thirteen-year-old son go on a plane alone didn't sit well with me but Jacob loved it.

We had finally spoken to Jacob about Joel being his biological father. He had surprised us both by taking it all in his stride. He had been inquisitive, even taking to listening to The Riots' music; but in his heart Daniel was still his dad, much to Daniel's relief. Despite his young age, Jacob had a much older head on his shoulders–something he surely had learnt from Daniel and not me.

This was only the second year of the custody arrangement and I had missed Jacob like crazy. I knew he would come home tanned and healthy looking while I still looked like a ghost with my pale skin and dark circles under my eyes from not sleeping without him in the house with me. I cried almost every day he was gone. He was almost a teenager now and I was starting to wonder how I'd cope when he eventually went off to college.

Loneliness engulfed me, although I'd always tried hard to keep that from Jacob. The last thing I'd wanted was for him to feel guilty about staying with his dad. Daniel regularly called to try and convince me that I should move closer to him. I couldn't imagine myself living anywhere else though.

Glancing out of the window, I could see that a plane had landed and my heart fluttered, hoping that it was Jacob's flight. I couldn't wait to give him a hug and check that he'd been eating well, even though I knew that Daniel and his new wife wouldn't see him go hungry. Jake would always be my baby boy though.

As I peered out of the expansive window overlooking the busy runway my phone started to ring. I moved to one side, away from the busy hustle and bustle of the airport and took my phone out of my pocket.

Jake's number flashed up on the screen and my heart jumped with excitement and anticipation. I wondered how my own mother could have abandoned me when I felt so tied to Jacob in every possible way. I shrugged off the thought and swiped the screen to answer his call.

"Baby, are you here? I can't see you," I chirped excitedly into the phone, a huge grin on my face.

"I'm delayed Ma, I won't be getting in until tomorrow," I heard him smile into the phone, his voice had started to break and I had noticed the deepness in it grow over the weeks we'd been apart and talking on the phone. "Dad got tickets for a really cool computer game show but it's only on today…"

My heart sank. I was mildly aware of a tinge of annoyance at the edge of my upset; surely Jacob or Daniel could have let me know before I'd driven to the airport and gotten myself all worked up.

"I need you to do me a favour though Ma," he continued, not waiting for me to respond. "I'm sorry I couldn't call earlier but since you're already there I wonder if you could pick up my friend. His flight should have just landed and he's from town."

"Oh, okay – I guess that's alright. How will I know who he is?" I talked into the cell phone and tried to hide the disappointment–and slight frustration–from my voice as the smile fell from my face.

"Oh, you'll know him when you see him Ma," Jake sounded excited and nervous which, which in turn made me curious. "Ma–I love you, I want you to be happy. Don't forget. I'll see you tomorrow."

Before I had the chance to answer, he was gone. I looked down at my phone and wondered to myself what on earth he was up to. It crossed my mind that he hadn't mentioned any of his friends were away for the summer and I glanced around, trying to see if I could spot a gawky teenager loitering around on their own.

I didn't have much chance to dwell on Jacob's call or my own disappointment because as soon as I looked around I could see what my not-so-little boy had been up to. But... how?

Stood looking right at me across the arrivals lounge was a face I hadn't seen in the flesh for almost six years. He was still as handsome, just a little worn around the edges now. His tired face lit up when our eyes met across the crowded space.

Joel hesitated only for a second before rushing to me and pulling me into a tight embrace. I shook with emotion; tears pouring down my face and I felt a lump lodge in my throat as I gulped for air. He was kissing my neck and cheek and I felt his tears mingle with my own.

"What... how?" I gasped, pulling away and putting a hand to my mouth in surprise.

"Jacob was in California and he asked to meet me. I didn't know his da... Daniel was living there now?" Joel started to explain. "Or that he knew, you know, about me."

"Daniel moved a couple of years ago and Jake stays with him for the summer. He contacted you?" I could barely stand, my legs were like jelly and so he put his arm around me and guided me over to the bank of seats so we could sit down.

"I'm not sure how he found my number but I went to meet him. I thought something had happened to you." He was holding my hand and sitting so close we could almost be conjoined. "He said his dad was married and he was staying with him but you were here alone. He came right out and asked if I was married or with anyone; which I'm not."

"He what? Oh my goodness – I'm sorry, Jacob likes to fix people. I'm so embarrassed," I could feel my cheeks start to flush.

I knew that Jake hated to leave me alone but I kept on reminding him that I was on my own because I chose to be. Letting Joel leave the second time had been my choice; I knew then that I would always love him, but there had been no place in his crazy rock-star life for Jake and I. As much as it had hurt, I knew that I couldn't be with him and give Jacob the stable life he deserved.

"I'm glad he found me; he's grown into a great young man. He is so much like you." Joel laughed, the smile lighting up his face as he did so. "He asked me to come and I didn't hesitate to say yes. It was really amazing to get to know him a little better."

I knew that he would see the doubt in my eyes. Although I knew that The Riots aren't together anymore and hadn't been for a few years from what I could gather from the magazines I scanned in the local shop, I wondered if the media circus is any less insane than it was six years earlier. Billy had exchanged some emails but we didn't talk about his life as much as we did about Jacob and so I didn't really know what he and Joel had been up to.

Admittedly I had seen and heard less and less of them in the media since Waz's death, but the insane world Billy and Joel inhabited was still no place for my young son.

"It isn't like it was. People recognise me, sure, but the reporters aren't interested in me anymore. I can walk down the street without having my picture splashed across the tabloids. I try to keep myself to myself and so the press have no interest anymore, I'm old news." He entwined his fingers with my own and kissed my hand, it was almost as though he was afraid I might blow away if he didn't keep hold of me. "I don't want that life Indi, I want you – wherever or however that might be, and I would really like to be a part of Jacob's life."

"I missed you so much," I cried hard. Years of heartache poured down my face like a river whose dam had just burst. "I didn't want to walk away from you but that was no life for Jake. It wasn't a life I wanted for myself either. I love you so much, I always have. It took everything to walk away from you that day; if not for Jacob I wouldn't have had the strength."

"Will you have me?" he asked. "Not just for a little bit, but for always?"

I laughed, snorting as I did.

"What's so funny?" he smiled at me, blushing slightly.

I laughed harder then. "That sounded so cheesy Joel! Have you started writing love songs or something?"

"Hey, I was having a moment!" he nudged me in the side with his elbow but grinned at me still.

"I'm sorry, it just sounded so unlike your rock star image!" I pulled him into a hug, intoxicated by the smell and feel of him.

We sat there in the middle of the busy airport holding each other and laughing, our heads bowed close together as we took each other in. It felt like home.

"Yes, I'll have you–forever," I told him.

If you enjoyed this book, please help an indie author out by leaving a review. You can leave one on Laura's Amazon page by using this universal link – myBook.to/RiotGirl

Please feel free to post a comment or stop by on any of the following:

www.laurawhiskenswriter.com

www.facebook.com/laurawhiskenswriter

www.twitter.com/whiskens83

Made in the USA
Charleston, SC
05 August 2015